A DEATH IN NEWPORT

MICHAEL HOGAN

D1502813

A DEATH IN NEWPORT

ISBN 13: 978-1463530822

Cover photo "Stoneacre Outbuildings" by Lucinda Mayo. Used with permission. Copyright © 2011 by Lucinda Mayo.

Published by Intercambio Press in cooperation with CreateSpace

For information on the author or any other inquiries, go to:
www.drmichaelhogan.com

A DEATH IN NEWPORT

MICHAEL HOGAN

A NOVEL

CHAPTER ONE

Newport, Rhode Island

It was August, the season of the Jazz Festival, tennis tournaments at the Casino, and sailing lessons on Narragansett Bay. The air was warm with a slight breeze, almost perfect, as tourists walked in the shade of two hundred year-old copper beeches and maples to visit the Marble Palace, Beechwood and the Breakers. When Michael Regan stepped out of the Pell Center in Newport, Rhode Island, he was upset and introspective. It had been a frustrating day.

The conference on Globalization and Religion had been dominated by Boston University professors, most of whom were proponents of unrestrained trade and development, regardless of social consequences. One professor in particular, Peter Bergman, author of several books on economics and sociology, had suggested that the reason for lack of development in Latin countries was their Catholic faith which had inculcated negative economic values, including "unrestrained fornication." Michael could not believe an enlightened intellectual could make such a statement in the 21st century and said so in no uncertain terms.

Still, it smarted. An Irish Catholic himself, he was an official member of the Bolivian delegation, one of the Latin American groups who had been invited to the conference. At first, he was honored to have been chosen to represent his university from Santa Cruz, Bolivia, but increasingly it was beginning to appear that the Central and South American professors were held in mild contempt by many of the presenters for their leftist views and their refusal to accept the globalization blueprint laid down by the most favored nations.

It was only seven o'clock. Too early to return to his room in the converted carriage house on the Salve Regina campus, plus he was still upset and would not properly digest his evening meal if he went home right away. So, he headed down Ruggles Avenue toward the Cliff Walk. The occasional cars that passed him as he walked by the tennis courts and the school of music were those of tourists or summer students. They courteously pulled to the center of the road to give him space, one couple waved. But he was too preoccupied to notice.

The waterfront trail that he followed passed the summer mansions of the Astors and the Vanderbilts but also traversed some of the most breathtaking coastal scenery in New England. In the first days of the conference he had walked a few short stretches of it, especially at the easier well-paved end which led to Easton's Beach. This time as he passed the Breakers on his left, he turned right, and headed down the southern end of the trail which had several more precipitous paths. That direction also involved a bit of climbing over boulders and through a tunnel or two, but it suited his mood. He needed to walk off some of his frustration.

It had been a fairly warm day but now the air was cooling and he walked at a brisk pace as the sun faded behind the trees and darkness crept up. With it, a mist and then a fog began to roll in and he heard the cries of gulls he couldn't see, and a fog horn off toward the Point.

As he approached the tunnel leading to the Chinese tea house, he was suddenly aware that his vision had become very limited. In the tunnel he felt a twinge of fear; he could see only a few inches ahead. He thought about turning back. It would be so easy to be assaulted here and to be left robbed and bleeding while the assailant disappeared in the night. But then he saw the brightening of the other end, dismissed his fears as foolish, and continued on. This was Newport, after all, not some inner city crime zone.

When he reached Rough Point, a promontory of granite and sedimentary rock, he was out of breath and paused to rest on a rock outcrop just above the path. He had managed during the walk to exorcize the negative feelings from the conference. He told himself that tomorrow was another day, and there would be many opportunities to put forth his points of view and those of his delegation. After a brief respite he rose to head back to the path. It was then that he saw a young man coming across the cliff with fishing gear.

"Buenas noches," the youngster said. Before the professor could even reply or reflect on how odd it was to hear Spanish in this locale, he was slammed on the side of his head with a heavy blow from the fishing pole the young man carried. Michael staggered backward, bewildered, slipped off the rock and fell to the roiling sea thirty feet below, where his spine was crushed on the jagged boulders. The fisherman disappeared into the night, while the waves smashed Michael's helpless body repeatedly against the rocks, and the tide rushed in on the cold Atlantic shore.

CHAPTER TWO

Guadalajara, Mexico

Gary Regan was playing his second set against Elias Ramirez, a fellow pro at the San Javier Country Club. The air at six thousand feet was cool but heavy with moisture. It was the rainy season and clouds from the early morning rain had not quite dissipated. Gary had won the first set handily 6-2, but in the second set he was down 1-3 because of a break in his concentration.

Working as an instructor at a tennis club in Mexico was not Gary's life goal. He had been on the Davis Cup team in his twenties and was even ranked in the top three hundred internationally. He had played in the Australian and the U.S. Open, but a couple of nagging injuries and abuse of prescription drugs had hurt his game and ultimately sidelined him permanently like Martina Hingis. He really admired Martina, even at her age, the reach to volley, cutting off the court, dominating the younger players. Although he was never ranked as high as her, drugs had effectively ended both their careers. It was a shame.

Gary had a degree in Spanish and Portuguese from Yale. So after washing out on the tennis circuit, he had parlayed the Yale degree into a job at a New England prep school. But booze and the night life got him dismissed from that as well. He moved to Mexico to take some graduate courses in Latin American history at the Universidad de Guadalajara. It was there he met, and fell in love with, his wife Teresa. Now, in his fourth year of drug-free sobriety he coached a little tennis, played a few games here and there with a local pro, and waited for his next big chance. At forty, the odds were slim that there would be a next big chance, but it didn't hurt to dream.

Gary knew he was a disappointment to his father. The head of economics at the Universidad Privada de Santa Cruz, Michael Regan hoped that his son would find his way to university career. When that did not happen, he gave his whole-hearted support to Gary playing on the tennis circuit. When Gary blew that, the professor pulled strings with ex-governor Whitman and Senator Pell from Rhode Island to get him a job at St. George's Preparatory School. When he failed in that as well, the professor pretty much gave up. Gary and his father had not communicated in years. Gary had not even told him that he had gotten into a Twelve Step program, given up booze and drugs, and was coaching tennis. There seemed no point.

Speaking of points…he realized he would not make any unless he gave up these self-recriminations and returned to the game. *Concentrate*, he told himself.

He had noticed that Ramirez, a left-handed player, had a tendency to lean toward the baseline when receiving. So, Gary delivered a slicing serve to the outside which Ramirez returned with a weak volley and Gary put that away easily. He kept it up, alternating serves and changing pace, rushing the net whenever the Mexican's volley was tentative. In fifteen minutes he was up 5-3. *If only life were like tennis,* he thought. If focus and concentration paid off, then he would certainly recoup his losses in life as well. Sure he had made some mistakes; he had been self-indulgent and lazy. But now, if he applied himself and concentrated, he could still make something of his life.

Ramirez served the last game and made a double fault. He had lost concentration and now Gary began springing up and down on his toes as he awaited the next serve. He anticipated the ball's arc, confidently caught as it rose, and slammed it back to the line at Ramirez's feet. Love-thirty. The next serve was a fault, the follow-up was tentative and Gary slammed it straight down the line before Ramirez could even get into position.

The final point was close, but an extended volley left Ramirez in the back court, and Gary sliced a drop shot just over the net for the win.

He took a shower and then went to check his email in the office. It was mostly spam which he quickly eliminated, but there was one odd email which he almost deleted but then decided out of curiosity to open. The caption was "Sad news…." It was from a friend, Carolina McGuire, his former high school Spanish teacher in Newport, whose husband was a police detective.

Dear Gary,

I was saddened to learn of the death of your father yesterday here in Newport. Please let me know when you get into town. My thoughts and my prayers go out to you at this difficult time. Carolina P.S. Feel free to call me at the office. (401) 846-8899.

Gary called her immediately and found out what little she knew from the article in the *Newport Daily News* and the few things her husband had told her. It wasn't much. Then he called the Newport Police Department and discovered from Detective McGuire that they had found his father's body, battered by rocks and tide, on a small beach off the Cliff Walk early yesterday morning. It had been in the water for six to eight hours according to the coroner's estimate. There was no immediate evidence of foul play. It appeared that he had simply fallen from a promontory in an especially perilous section of the Cliff Walk while hiking in the fog. Gary told McGuire he would be on the next available plane.

When he got home, his wife Teresa had already been on the phone with officials in Santa Cruz, Bolivia. Teresa, a slim brunette with quick intelligent eyes, now saddened by the news of his father's death, met him at the door. She gave him a long hug and held him in her arms.

"I'm so sorry, Gary. They called me from Bolivia with the news. What can I do to help?"

Gary explained briefly what he had learned from Newport and that it was imperative he go there as soon as possible. He wondered if Teresa could arrange her schedule so that she could go to Bolivia and take care of his father's estate. Teresa worked as a free lance translator so her hours were generally flexible.

"No problem," she said. "I'll book both our flights on-line. Just let me have your credit card." Gary gave her the card and she headed into her office.

"Listen, while I'm doing that, Gary, why don't you make a call to the lawyer over at the tennis club, what his name, Licenciado Diaz? Let him know what's going on, and see if he can draw up a power of attorney so that I can sign whatever papers are necessary for your Dad's will and pick up his personal effects down in Bolivia. Then make a pot of coffee and unwind a bit out in the back garden. I'm sure none of this has really sunk in yet. You need some time alone to sort things out."

CHAPTER THREE

Houston, Texas

The two-hour flight to Houston on Continental's Embraer jet was quick and uneventful. But walking from the plane to immigration up one long corridor, down another, up one ramp then across a quarter mile passageway, made Gary feel like the plane had landed on the Mexican side of the border and that he was crossing on foot into Texas. Once at Passport Control, the lines stretched for four rows of arrivals each a hundred yards long, and those were only the U.S. passport holders. The Visitors' lines were even longer. When Gary finally got up to the final lane and looked at his watch he noted that he had less than forty minutes to make his connection. If all went well and he could get his luggage and check through customs with no problems, he might still make it.

He presented his passport to the agent, a buffed specimen in his mid-thirties who looked like he should be doing something more physical with his life, maybe playing middle linebacker for the Houston Oilers, but certainly not sitting behind a computer. He'd looked at Gary's document. It was a passport from the Consulate in

Mexico where he last renewed it, so it did not have the coded magnetic bar to swipe as passports issued in the U.S. do. The agent tapped the numbers into his computer. He looked at the computer for a full five minutes. Then, he tapped some more numbers into the computer. Then he looked up at Gary.

"You know you're on the watch list?" he asked looking as if Gary was guilty of *something* but he didn't know what exactly.

"Yes, Gary said. I *do* know that. I've been on that list for six years for no good reason that anyone can determine. Maybe I have the same name as an IRA terrorist or something. At any rate, when you check the birth date, I come away cleared every time."

"So, you live in Mexico, do ya?" He asked, paging through the entry and exit visas in the booklet.

"Yes."

"What kind of work do you do down there."

"I'm a tennis instructor."

"Hmm. So, how did you end up with a passport issued by the Consulate?"

Gary thought about responding that when one lives in Mexico, the U.S. Consulate is where passport renewal takes place. But he felt that with this particular agent one question would simply lead to another. "Look, is this going to take long? I only have fifteen minutes to make my flight"

"I don't think you'll make your flight, sir. Would you mind stepping out of line?"

Another agent appeared from beyond the cubicle and escorted Gary to a small room where he was thoroughly searched, then asked a number of questions about his work and the purpose of his visit. They checked his FM3 Mexican working papers, asked about his last IRS filing (it was current), and then entered more numbers and data into a computer. When Gary was finally allowed to go and get his luggage, he found that it had been thoroughly searched as well. He also had missed his connection to Providence.

He took his suitcase through customs, gave the officer the signed form, and then put the bag on the conveyor belt for the in-transit flight. There was no point in hurrying now. He'd have to exit the security area anyway, so at first he thought he'd get a bite to eat. Then, as he passed an airport bar and felt the return of that old urge he'd get whenever he became too frustrated or angry, he decided on the lesser of two evils. He went and bought a pack of Marlboro Lights and then, since he had to exit the security area anyway to rebook the second leg of his flight, headed out to the parking ramp and the smoking section with the rest of the non-conformists, losers, and geriatric addicts.

He smoked two cigarettes and thought about his dad. He felt no grief or sense of loss just yet. Perhaps that would come later. Right now his mind was full of details: wondering what he'd say at the memorial service, thinking about who he needed to contact to let them know the news. His mother had been dead for ten years now and Gary was the only child. But his grandmother was still alive. Although since she lived in Newport, he was sure she had already been notified. She would have been listed as next of kin and the police knew that and would have gone by to see her. Other than that, there were his father's colleagues at work, and his father's old friend Noam Chomsky at M.I.T. His father had a pretty full life and, while sixty-four was young to die in this century of extended care and modern medicine, Gary took comfort in the fact that his father had managed to avoid the indignities of old age. He died at the peak of his professional life at a major international conference. And, the slip from the Cliff Walk, while perhaps briefly painful, was sudden and final. There were worse ways to die, Gary thought, and he heard of many of them at AA meetings.

At least his father had done something with his life. That was the important thing. Standing here in a stinking parking garage, inhaling the exhaust fumes of cars and taxis, smoking a Marlboro Light, sweating in the Houston humidity, Gary asked himself what he had done with his own life. If he were to die tomorrow, who would even speak at his funeral? He had no son, nobody with whom he worked who would find much good to say about him. Besides Teresa, the few people he knew in Guadalajara didn't speak any English, so even if they knew him well enough to give a eulogy, they would not have the words and there would be no one to listen.

But this isn't about me, he checked himself. *It's about the old man.* So, he made a note to contact Chomsky and see if he'd have a few words to say, and then some of his father's colleagues from Bolivia. Then he thought he'd contact the newspapers and see if he could get a good obituary in the *Providence Journal* and maybe even the *Times.* He believed that those efforts, though meager, might at least ease his grandmother's pain at her son's passing.

CHAPTER FOUR

Providence

Seven hours later, after a quick stopover in Newark, Gary arrived a bit frazzled and nicotine-depleted at Rhode Island's T.F. Green airport. The only state-owned airport in the U.S., it was bright, efficient and relatively uncrowded—a welcome relief after the crowds at Houston and Newark.

He was about to head for the baggage pickup when he heard someone call his name. He turned and there were the McGuires.

"You guys!" he said after he had hugged Carolina and shaken hands with her detective husband, an ex-Marine who, although closer to Gary's dad's age than his own, still did fifty pushups each morning and was an expert on the pistol range. "How the hell did you know when I was coming in, Pete? My plane was delayed."

Pete shrugged as if it was no big deal. "I have a friend on the Houston P.D. He told me that the sergeant at the airport noticed that Homeland security had delayed your departure. So, I called and found out the arrival time of the next flight."

"*Pobrecito*," Carolina murmured. "*¿Como estás?*" Carolina asked

12

"Never mind the Spanish," Pete growled. "We're in Providence not L.A."

"Well, this is Warwick, actually, *mi amor*," quipped Carolina, who despite her diminutive stature could still effectively counter the bulk of her husband's two hundred-pound intimidation. "But, you're right. English. So, how is it going? How are you coping?'

"All right," Gary said. "Maybe it really hasn't kicked in yet. Maybe we've been apart for so long that I really don't know what I feel. On the flight up here I've actually been feeling more self-pity than grief. I mean, my old man had accomplished quite a bit in his life. He was respected in his profession, pretty well-known internationally, he published lots of articles, and in the end died from a fall, quick and sudden. I wish we could have come together before that happened, but then again, it probably wouldn't have made much difference. I disappointed him most of his life, and would have disappointed him at the end as well. A failed tennis player. Not much you can say about that."

"Well, you're right about the self-pity business," Pete interrupted. "You need to get over all that, dude. Listen, let's go get a drink."

"I gave up the booze three years ago, Pete. How about a cup of coffee?"

"Even better," Pete said. "I want to talk to you about your dad's accident. Some of the details are a bit puzzling."

They each ordered the brew of the day, a Honduran blend, at the coffee shop. Pete took his coffee black, but Carolina and Gary fussed over the Half and Half and sugar while Pete got them a table and waited impatiently. When they got seated and Carolina had passed them each a napkin, Pete began.

"Listen, as of this moment, nothing that I say is anything more than speculation. So, let me just lay it out for you. When the receiving physician first examined the body, there was no question in his mind that it was simply an accident. Your dad slipped on a dangerous portion of the Cliff Walk and fell to his death. It was a foggy night, the cliffs were wet. It would have been easy to lose one's footing in the fog, slip on a wet patch, and…gone."

"What are you saying, Pete? Has something changed since then?"

Pete sipped his coffee, looked at Carolina and then nodded. "If you and Carolina were not such good friends, I wouldn't be here telling you this. We don't usually share details of a pending investigation with the bereaved. But she suggested that we come pick you up, and she thinks that you can handle it."

"Handle what?" Gary asked fumbling with a cigarette and a box of matches.

"You can't light that in here, Gary. This isn't Mexico," Pete snapped. "We've got laws."

"Okay, okay. Jesus. You sound like you've been watching too much Lou Dobbs, for Chrissake. We have laws in Mexico, too. Just not as many as you do in the land of the free.

"Well, anyway, I do some background investigation in any violent death. I checked with the Pell Center to find out if your Dad was depressed or if he had been drinking. You know. Anything that might lead to an accident or even a suicide? There was nothing. He was very active, positive.

"And he doesn't drink. He never did."

"Yeah, I found that out as well. I also discovered that he had several heated discussions with a professor from Boston University. I learned that there were other people at the conference who objected to your father's presence there. It seems that he was very tight with Chávez in Venezuela and helped him set up a regional bank which kind of pissed off U.S. investors. One professor even referred to him as a Marxist, and said it set a bad precedent for your dad to be invited."

"But professors don't go around bumping each other off," Gary said.

"Who says? Remember the Bay of Pigs? Several of those guys were former professors who left the country when Castro took power. How about the Arab doctors in London who were arrested after plotting a bombing? There are extremists on all sides of this globalization issue. Social position, academic degree, even wealth, doesn't necessarily eliminate someone from extremism. Osama Bin Laden, for example, is a multi-millionaire of the highest class among the Saudis. Besides, one of them could have paid to have it done. How much would it cost to get some biker to follow your dad down the cliff and give him a shove? A couple of hundred bucks? A couple of grams of crystal meth?"

"A biker?"

"Well, that's just a thought. There were several in town for the music festivals out at Fort Adams State Park. We gave their Harleys a police escort down Belleview and around the Ocean Drive but that doesn't mean one of them couldn't have dropped out of the line.

"Anyway, to get back to my original point. Your dad's body wasn't too banged up or bloated. We found the corpse on a small beach less than a few hundred yards from where he fell, or was pushed. A small cove. His spine was broken and some ribs where he went backwards off the cliff. Now that in itself is fairly unusual. People usually don't fall backwards off cliffs. No real evidence of foul play, but enough to justify further investigation.

"Now this is where it gets interesting. When the first examination was done at Newport Hospital, the doctor there signed the death certificate and the medical examiner just stamped it: 'Accidental death.' I was doing some preliminary investigation like I said, but I was called off the case. I was told it was an accident and we didn't need any follow up. I was also told that I had been asked to give a lecture at Roger Williams University and that preparing for it had top priority because it was one of the ex-governor's projects and he especially asked for me.

Carolina pulled at his sleeve and he nodded. "This is where I come in. I got a call from my friend Carla, who works part-time at O'Neill's Funeral Home. She told me that something occurred which was kind of strange and she wanted to know what I thought about it. Seems that they intended to cremate Michael Regan's body later that afternoon."

"Cremate him!" Gary interrupted. "My grandmother would never go for that. All the Regans are buried out at St. Columba's. We have a specially reserved plot on the hillside overlooking the harbor."

"I know that, and I told her so. She said that's what she thought too. So, that's when I called Pete. He was over at the library on Spring Street working on his lecture but feeling kind of put out and preoccupied. He knew that if it was a homicide the investigators really needed to do everything they could in the first 48 hours or otherwise the likelihood of solving it would be severely diminished."

Pete finished his coffee. "So, let's get your bag and then you can go and have a cigarette. We can finish this up outside. You look like you need that smoke."

Pete grabbed Gary's suitcase off the half-empty carrousel and Gary followed him outside. He lit up a cigarette and offered one to Pete and Carolina as well. Pete looked at the pack wistfully but declined. Carolina took a cigarette and Gary lit them both on the same match.

"So," Pete continued. "I went to the morgue to make a closer examination of the body and take some notes. First, his spine was broken, like I said earlier, and some ribs were busted as well. Both injuries appeared to be a result of the fall from the cliff. Second, except for a couple of pecks from gulls, his face and head were pretty clean. No bruises, marks, lacerations or even much bloating. There was, however, one substantial swelling and a break in the skin just over his right ear at the hairline which I had not noticed earlier during my cursory examination at the scene. It was made by a rounded instrument such as a small club, or maybe the handle of a fishing rod wielded with some force and leverage. So I called the medical examiner back. I went over the evidence with him and he said he would change his notation to 'Death by Misadventure' which includes accident, of course, but keeps the possibility of homicide open. I also asked him to do a complete battery of tests, blood, toxicology screen, DNA, the works.

"Then I got a call from the station. I was told to head on out to my lecture at the university up in Bristol, and then report to the FBI office in Providence where they want me to work as a liaison on some organized crime task force. I ask the chief *What about this Michael Regan thing?* And he tells me, *That's been resolved. The family wants it closed, and without any real suspect, or any real evidence, there's no reason to keep it open.* So I tell him about the blow to the side of the head, and he says that could just as easily have happened in the water. And I said that was unlikely because a rock would make a jagged cut not a rounded knob and then he said, *Pete, you want to keep your job? Let it go. This case is closed.*"

"So, what now?" Gary asked as they headed across the long expanse of the Newport Bridge and looked down at the lights of a forty-foot yacht cruising below.

Carolina turned around in her seat and grasped his hand. "Now, you spend the next couple of nights at our place. Snoop around, talk to your grandmother, and find out what you can about why everyone wants to close this case. Pete will be working with the Feds up in Providence but he'll call every day."

"They can't pull *you* off the case," Pete said, taking the exit for downtown Newport. "You're his son, after all. If it was murder, then maybe you'll turn up something. Bring it to a head. On the other hand, maybe there's nothing to find. Maybe it was a just a freak accident and that's the end of it."

"In that case, it will still be worthwhile," Carolina said. "You'll see where your father passed his final days, come to know him a bit more, and get to grieve."

Gary was quiet in the backseat. His stomach had begun to cramp and he once again began to feel that familiar sense of being in over his head, beyond his depth. He was unqualified temperamentally to cross-examine his father's colleagues or even his own grandmother. He was unequipped emotionally to deal with any members of his family. He needed an AA meeting. He wanted a cigarette. He wished he was back in Mexico.

CHAPTER FIVE

Gary had trouble going to sleep in the McGuires' guest room. Although was exhausted from his journey, the delays and questioning in Houston, he kept going over the new revelations about his father's death. Was it, in fact, a homicide? Who could be behind it? And what could be the motive? He had been so distant from his father for the past several years that he only knew what he read in political journals or on the Internet.

He knew that, although his father was ostensibly an economics professor, he had actively worked with several South American governments. He knew that he was one of the architects of the Bolivarian Revolution championed by Hugo Chávez as both a unifying and leftward movement of the region's republics. He suspected that there were people in Washington who were not comfortable with that. However, his father had not been connected with any violent movements or conspiracies. Quite the opposite, in fact. He had worked to make societies more equal, to draw up plans in Bolivia to distribute lands which had been in the hands of a few powerful families for centuries, to strengthen the miners' unions, and to expand public education and health. He had used his contacts with the Chávez government to secure low interest loans from Venezuela to Bolivia and to set up the regional bank.

Gary checked his watch. It was now 5 AM and he decided to get up and take a little walk down to the harbor. He dressed in tan slacks, a blue work shirt, and tennis shoes. Then he crept quietly down the back stairs and out onto Warner Street. It was quiet and there was a cool fog off the ocean which muffled even the occasional car that passed up on Broadway. He slowed after passing Farewell Street and looked down from the overpass into the graveyard below. He thought about the transitory nature of life, and how many more people there were in the earth than on top of it, despite the billions who struggled each day to survive. He thought about the futility of it all. What did it matter in the end? The tennis bum who scratched and shuffled from one low paying gig to another. The brilliant professor who worked to provide the poor with a decent way of life. They both ended up in the same place. Mother Teresa's body was eaten by worms just like Saddam Hussein's.

He lit a cigarette and then followed Elm Street to the Wellington Street Pier. He looked out over the skeleton of the Newport Bridge rising from the mist and saw an elusive beauty there, although it was misleading. The majestic bridge, more than anything else, had turned Newport from a quiet and remote island into a tourist spot with day-trippers from New York and Boston clogging the cobblestone streets. Out on Goat Island, which used be the Naval Torpedo Station during the war, was a $400 a night Hyatt Regency where visitors who could not afford the exorbitant rent on a summer home usually stayed. Four hundred dollars. That was enough money to keep a Mexican family of five for a month. For a Bolivian farm worker it was six months' salary. Even poor people in the United

States were rich by comparison with most of the world, but few Americans knew or cared.

A sound echoed from the far side of the bridge and he looked over to Coaster's Island. The light had come on signaling reveille at the Naval War College. He remembered his father telling him that in the 1800s, before the Navy took it over, it was the County Insane Asylum. Some irony there, but he had neither the inclination nor the energy to explore it this morning.

He sat on a wooden bench for a few minutes but then the damp and the cold drove him to continue his walk. As he headed up the hill toward the McGuires he passed a number of signs advertising the real estate company which was co-owned by his aunt Victoria. Regan and Stein. They seemed to be doing a good business, especially with the restored Colonials in this section of town, some of which had price tags in the millions. Victoria had always been the kind of entrepreneur who saw opportunities just a beat before the rest of the crowd and seized them and her profits while others were still looking around. She was the one who convinced the Bouviers to have their daughter's wedding at St. Mary's Church in Newport despite Joe Kennedy's insistence that it be held at the cathedral in Boston where his old friend Archbishop Cushing presided. She made a small fortune on the decorations, flowers, catering, and guest services which she helped coordinate for political and business leaders who attended the nuptials from all over the world. She helped put the Redwood Library on the map as the most prestigious subscription library in New England, despite the rather small collection and limited outreach facilities, convincing the wealthy that it was more exclusive and discriminating.

She helped fight off McDonalds and Walmart and other lowbrow developers who tried unsuccessfully to move into the

Bellevue district, and organized a coalition of business leaders to remodel and lease to high-end shops and develop estate tax foreclosures into expensive condos. She worked with Jimmy Van Allen to make the Newport Casino, a run-down relic of a bygone era, into a vibrant and financially successful Tennis Hall of Fame. Gary had a great deal of respect for her, but she had little for him or his father, and he had not spoken to her in years.

Her friendship with the former governor had not hurt either. Her refusal to even speak to Gary after his last sacking was not something he blamed her for. She saw him as someone who betrayed the family and whose feckless behavior, drinking and drugging, had tarnished the family name. She would not welcome him home and would prefer that he leave as soon as possible after the funeral.

Pete McGuire's suggestion that he further investigate the facts of his father's death failed to take any of this into account. Gary was *persona non grata* in this town. Besides the McGuires and maybe his grandmother, he could think of no one who would even give him the time of day.

He smelled coffee as he came in the door and the rich odor of sizzling bacon. Carolina was in the kitchen, which opened off the back hallway, stirring scrambled eggs. She was dressed in jeans, a white blouse, with a flowered apron around her waist. Her gray hair was pulled back off her neck and she looked refreshed and younger than her sixty-odd years.

"Hi, Gary! Out for a walk? Have a seat and I'll get your coffee. We don't usually have a heavy breakfast, mostly just fruit and cereal. But with Pete driving up to Providence and you going out early, I figured you could both use something a bit more substantial." She poured the coffee and set the cream and sugar in front of him. "So, where did you go? Just a walk?"

22

"Down to the pier on Wellington. I woke up early and thought I'd stretch my legs and think things over a bit."

"And what did you decide?" she asked, placing the plates of crisp bacon and scrambled eggs on the table.

"That I wouldn't be of much use with Pete's investigation. I mean, my aunt doesn't even talk to me anymore. And Grandma Regan is as tight-lipped as they come, even though she does have a warm place in her heart for me."

"Well, that's where you start. From what I gather, she's going to have a wake after all, a Mass at St. Augustine's and the burial in the family plot in St. Columba's. I hear the Kennedys sent their condolences, and probably Representative Patrick Kennedy will come down from the capitol to escort your famous aunt.

"Yep, that's right," Pete called as he came into the kitchen after giving a quick glance in the hall mirror to straighten his tie. "Heck, even the Clintons might show up. They were good friends of ex-governor Whitman and he's always had a close connection with your family."

"Yeah," said Gary, with a scowl. "The noblesse oblige sort of connection."

"Whatever," replied Pete, beginning to get annoyed with Gary's negativity. "Finish your breakfast and then get out there and see what you can find. The time for sulking is over. Here are the keys to the Chevy. I'm taking the Jetta. Be as cynical as you want, son, but keep your eyes and your ears open. It's going to be a tough week for everyone."

CHAPTER SIX

Bellevue Avenue

Tommy the Ragman pushed his shopping cart down Bellevue. It was still early and he hoped to get it off the main drag before the cops pulled him over. They didn't like to see him pushing his load of cans, bottles and dumpster-pickings down Bellevue during the high tourist season. But if he could get down Ruggles before eight o'clock, he could hide the cart behind some hedges, and then explore the Cliff Walk from there to Bailey's Beach for flotsam.

When he heard the whoop-whoop of the police car, he quickly turned on Narragansett, his heart beating wildly. It was too early to get stopped by the local police; he had just opened his hair-of-the-dog bottle of wine and did not want to lose it. He looked back and saw the patrolman had stopped a green Chevy, so he hustled past the old St. Catherine's School to go the back route through Salve Regina University to Ruggles Ave. *No sense taking any chances.*

When he got to the University soccer field he concealed his cart in a corner of the privet hedge, pulled out a heavy duty plastic garbage bag and headed for the ocean. Tommy was in his early sixties but he could easily pass for eighty. The sun and weather, and years of cheap wine, had weathered his skin and clouded his eyes.

There were some men cutting grass on the north end of the field and he thought about saying something to them about his cart. Years ago, when this was part of the Whitman estate there would have been no problem. He'd just tell the head gardener or one of his assistants to keep his eye on it for him. But now there weren't any head gardeners left. The Catholic Church, the University and the Preservation Society had bought up all the old estates. The taxes got too high for even the Vanderbilts and Astors. Now they all used landscape companies and contractors, many of them not even local, to prune the trees and cut the lawn.

Still, there wasn't much to steal from his cart. He had cashed in all the cans the night before at the recycling center, so that only left a ratty couple of blankets and an old *Playboy* he had picked out of a dumpster. He felt that today would be a good day, though. The wind was up last night and there were usually odd bits tossed up on the shore after an evening of high, rough seas. All kinds of things fell overboard as the sailing yachts battled to get back to safety. Even the power yachts sometimes ended up losing fishing gear, flotation cushions, and articles of clothing.

His best score was when he was just a kid. He and Billy Malone were out on the Ocean Drive when they saw these huge black bales floating in on the waves. They climbed down from the sea walls and hauled them up. They were bales of raw rubber lost when the *Andrea Doria* and the *Stockholm* crashed into each other and sank. The salvage company paid them $40 a piece for those bales. That was a lot of money back in the Fifties and, even though his Dad took most of it when he found out, he and Billy had a couple of great beer drunks off it.

That was the great adventure about being a scavenger, he reflected. *You never knew what you'd find.* He took a pull off his pint bottle of Thunderbird and walked down the cliff to the shore.

Gary had just passed De La Salle Academy, now converted to condominiums, when he heard the whoop of the police car. He had been fiddling with the radio, trying to find a decent Oldies station and looked up expecting the squad car to go past. Instead, the cop gestured for him to pull over. Out of the corner of his eye he noticed an old homeless man pushing a shopping cart. The old guy looked back at the cop, scared, and rapidly turned the corner onto Narragansett. *Jesus. Who would believe it? There are even street people in this town.*

He reached in his pocket and pulled out his license, then looked up into the rear mirror. The cop had not gotten out of the car. Instead he was talking into his radio and now he spoke through the car's loud speaker.

"Sir, please exit your vehicle and place your hands up on the roof."

What the hell? Gary wondered. Gary put his license back into his pocket and then got out of the car.

"Let me see your hands," the cop commanded over the loud speaker. "Put them on the roof of your vehicle."

The patrolman, a swarthy lad in his twenties came over, gave him a thorough pat-down and then asked him for his license.

"What is this about, officer?" Gary asked.

"Do you have the registration on this vehicle?" the policeman asked, ignoring his question.

"Yes, I do. It belongs to Lieutenant Pete McGuire who is on your force. His wife is my former high school teacher and he lent it to me. I'm here for my dad's funeral."

"Let's go back to my vehicle, Mr. Regan, and you can tell me a bit more about that. Your father is the professor who fell off the cliff, is that right?" he asked, putting Gary in the back seat and then typing some data into his dashboard computer.

"That's correct."

"And you know the Lieutenant, how?"

"His wife was my high school Spanish teacher. We've been friends for years."

"And where is the Lieutenant now?

"He's attending an FBI session in Providence and he took his Jetta. He let me have the Chevy."

The officer put Gary's license on a clipboard, wrote a few notes and then picked up the radio transmitter. "This is car twelve, Molly. I have a suspect in custody driving Lieutenant McGuire's Chevy. Can you call and confirm with Mrs. McGuire that…." He glanced down at the license on his clipboard, "That one Gary Regan has permission to use said vehicle?"

"Ten-four. Hold on."

CHAPTER SEVEN

Tommy walked down the tree-line avenue past the walled estates and turreted mansions. He kept his eyes open for anything of value by the side of the road and along the walkways, anything hidden in a crevice of the brick and mortar walls, or stuffed into litter barrels on the sidewalks. Pickings were slim. Tourists, especially in this part of town, seldom discarded anything. They were bussed here in groups, or came on the Newport Trolley to the Forty Steps which was a popular stop, or they went south on Ochre Court where the tour bus took them to the Breakers.

The best time for Tommy was in the fall when the students returned to Salve Regina. Then, since they were prohibited from drinking or smoking in the dorms, the students went for walks with their six-packs, their pints of Seagram's or Smirnoff's, and their packs of Marlboros. After they got their quick buzz and hurried back to campus before curfew, they often left behind half empty pints, full cans of beer, and almost-full packs of smokes. Tommy uncovered several such windfalls in every season except summer.

He paused beneath a spreading oak and picked up a couple of green acorns and dropped them into his pocket. *Nothing worthwhile along here*, he thought, but he continued to look behind each hedge compulsively as he continued on his way.

He was still shaking a bit from alcohol withdrawal and the close encounter with the cop who was so close Tommy was sure he was going to bust him with the borrowed shopping cart. Fortunately, he pulled a motorist over and now had bigger fish to fry. Tommy pulled his bottle of Thunderbird out of the paper sack. *Still half full.* He took a deep swig, shivered and gagged at the taste. He coughed compulsively, brought up some phlegm, and then held himself still as the vomit reflex slowly subsided along with the tremors.

Once he got to Ochre Court Ave, he'd be safe. The campus cops seldom bothered him. From there he'd cross to Ruggles and then turn on the Cliff Walk where he'd be hidden from the road.

He had recognized the cop. *Portuguese guy from Bristol by the name of Rego. "C. Rego" it said on his silver nametag. A wise-ass. Wonder what the C stood for? Clem? Cecil? Corky? Ha! Weren't hardly any Newport cops from Newport anyhow. Just a couple of old detectives like McGuire. All the junior cops were from out of town. Lived in barracks for Chrissakes. The city manager's way of avoiding any undue influence that locals might have. Stupid, if you ask me. Probably these days no one could afford to live in Newport on a cop's salary anyway.*

The little shack he lived in was actually one of the old tool sheds from Hugo Key's defunct landscaping business. That and the disability check he got from the government saw him through. But he was getting a lot of pressure lately. That Victoria bitch at the realty company was pressuring the owner to clear the land and list the property. If that happened, he would end up sleeping on the docks where he'd surely freeze to death once winter came.

- -

"Do you have a passport, Mr. Regan?" the policeman asked, his leather belt and attachments creaking as he turned to the screen that separated him from his prisoner in the backseat.

"Yes, here it is," Gary offered, taking the blue booklet out of his back pocket.

"Okay, open it up to the photo page, please, and hold it up against the security screen. Good."

The policeman copied the birth date and passport number onto the incident report on his clipboard.

"Okay. Now please turn to the visa page with the entry stamp and visa from immigration.

He picked up the cell phone which was vibrating on the dash. "Yes, Molly. Okay, that's fine. Would you tell her that she needs to catch a cab to Bellevue and Narragansett and pick up the car? As a courtesy to the Lieutenant I won't have it towed. That's right, the corner of Narragansett and Bellevue. I'll be waiting."

"What!" Gary yelped. "What the hell are you doing? You know that she said I have permission to use the car. So, why are you doing this?"

"I don't like your tone, Mr. Regan. So, sit back in your seat and get away from the screen. We can go down to the station if that's what you'd prefer and straighten it out there. No? Okay, then. Here's the deal. Yes, you had permission to use the car. That's not the problem. The problem is that you gave me a Guadalajara driver's license and an International Permit.

"Both valid and current."

"That's correct. They are valid for thirty days according to Rhode Island state law from the date of your passport entry. If a motorist stays any longer than that he must surrender both documents to the DMV, then take a written test, an eye exam, pay a fee and get a valid Rhode Island license."

"So? I've only been here twenty-four hours."

"Yes, but you obtained the license through fraudulent means. My check with the DMV showed me that you have a driving under the influence conviction and a license suspension from the Middletown P.D."

"But that was ten years ago!"

"About the time you got your Mexican license, correct?"

"Well, a few months later I was offered a job down in Guadalajara."

"How convenient. The fact remains, however, that the license was fraudulently obtained so I am confiscating it, along with your international permit. You may keep your passport as a means of identification. I'm letting you off easy because I know you had a death in the family and I also know that you're an old friend of the McGuires. But I'll tell you this. If I see you behind the wheel of a vehicle in Newport, I'll charge you with a felony. Is that clear?"

A cab pulled up behind the squad car with Carolina in the back. She paid off the driver and approached the cop. "What's going on, Officer Rego?"

"Hello, Mrs. McGuire. I'm afraid your friend was driving on an invalid Mexican license. I'm letting him go with a warning this time, as a professional courtesy to the Lieutenant. But he can't drive a vehicle in Newport during his stay here."

He got out of the car, opened the back door and let Gary out. "Watch your head, sir."

C .Rego, Gary noted as he looked up at the cop's silver ID pin beneath his badge. *Wonder what the C stands for? Cecil? Calvin. Clementine?*

31

He got into the passenger's side of the car and slammed the door. Carolina got behind the wheel but she waited until the cruiser drove off before starting her car.

"What was that all about?" she asked.

When he explained, she said, "That is such a crock. You could have easily applied for a re-instatement of driving privileges after the six months were up. What a jerk! Oh well. You can go by DVD later in the week and do that. In the meantime let's cruise down to the Pell Center. Dr. Alioto, the director, is a good friend of mine and he's got a touring bicycle that I'm sure he'll let you borrow for a few days. He's too busy to use it most days. Plus, we'll get him to introduce you to the panel at the globalization conference as soon as they have a break. All of them know your dad and one of them might provide you with a clue to his death."

"Thanks, Carolina. I'm sorry to be such trouble."

"No trouble at all, Gary. Let's just hope that something positive comes from all this."

"About that cop…Rego?"

"Young kid. His dad had a great old farm in Tiverton. Portuguese family that went back several generations. Anyway, the dad sold out to developers, then lost most of the money gambling up at Foxwoods. The kid did a tour in Iraq, came home and got the associates degree in law enforcement at Roger Williams, and settled in Bristol. Joined the force a couple of years ago. He's got a chip on his shoulder for Newporters, and especially for your Aunt Victoria, who was the one who persuaded his father to sell the farm."

"C. Rego. What does the C stand for?"

"Clem," Carolina smiled.

"As in Clementine."

"Don't go there," Carolina smiled.

"Or a boy named Sue. No wonder he's got an attitude."

CHAPTER EIGHT

They arrived at the well-manicured estate which housed the Pell Center for International Relations just as the panelists were taking their mid-morning break. Carolina introduced Gary to the director, Dr. Alioto, who was sipping coffee at his desk. Paul Alioto, a former pilot, now an author, professor and consultant on international security, looked both professorial and military. A receding hairline and graying beard barely gentled his penetrating and inquisitive eyes. *Here's a man who misses very little,* Gary thought.

He greeted Carolina as an old friend and offered them a choice of freshly-brewed Colombian coffee or Santorini water which they declined. He showed a genuine sadness when introduced to Gary and said, "I am so sorry for your loss. Professor Regan was a giant in his field."

They talked a little bit about the Center and his work there, as well as the most recent conference. Carolina told him about Gary's transportation problems and he offered not only his bicycle for transportation, but housing at one of the university residences for the duration of Gary's stay.

"Your father was staying in a lovely apartment at Stoneacre, which is a converted carriage house just down the road. You're certainly welcome to stay there for the remainder of the conference. Here, let me give you the keys right now. I'll call security and advise them that you're moving in."

"Thank you, that's very generous," Gary said accepting the keys. "I'm sure Carolina and her husband will be relieved, although she'd never say so."

"Gary, you know you can stay with us as long as you like!" Carolina protested.

"I know," Gary said, clasping Carolina's shoulder in a gesture of gratitude. "And I'm very appreciative of all you've done so far. But you and Pete have your own work and your life. This is a perfect solution."

"So, Dr. Alioto,"....

"Call me, Paul, please."

"Paul. Out of curiosity how did things go during my father's visit here? Were there any conflicts?

Alioto smiled. "Conflicts? Your father? Well, you know that Professor Regan was, how can I put it? A bit polemical? He naturally disagreed with most of the globalists."

"Anyone in particular?"

"Well, I suppose most of the dustups tended to include the Austrian professor, Peter Bergman, from Boston University. Dr. Bergman had some theories about the virtues of capitalism and the Protestant ethic which particularly annoyed your father."

"They argued?"

"Yes, quite a bit. As a matter of fact the day he, uh...passed away there was a particularly heated discussion. It seems that Bergman was contending that part of the failure of Latin American economies was that the populations were hamstringed by Catholicism. Not only had the Latins not developed the positive values of the Protestant reformation which Bergman submitted had led to the rise of capitalism in Western Europe, but they had embraced negative Catholic values which managed to stifle progress. One which particularly annoyed your father was what Bergman termed 'a tendency towards indiscriminate copulation.'"

"What?"

"Yes, an unfortunate comment. Bergman has a bit of the Austrian eugenicist in his character, I'm afraid. And it got worse from there. I remember after our meal your father was so angry he developed indigestion, so he decided to take a walk along the cliff to try to clear his head and let go of some of the anger. That was the last we heard of him until the police came to report his fall the next day."

"You're certain it was a fall. You don't think Bergman....?"

"Of course not. Professor Bergman is 75 years old and quite frail actually, although his tongue is still as barbed and his mind as sharp as it ever was. Plus, he was here most of the evening and I walked him to his quarters about nine. No, I suspect it is like the police said. An unfortunate accident. While there were many here who disagreed with your father, including me," he smiled apologetically, "no one wanted to do him in, if that's what you're thinking."

"Well, I don't know what to think, really. I've only just got here. It did seem like there was a bit of a rush to have him cremated."

"Hmm...I hadn't heard that. I'd guess someone gave you wrong information on that. In fact, what I did hear was that he was to be honored at a Mass at St. Augustine's and then interred at St. Colomba's. In fact, I was asked by Governor Whitman to help write the obituary. Here's the draft if you'd like to see it."

He produced a sheet of stationery with the Pell Center letterhead and placed it between Carolina and Gary so that both could read.

MICHAEL REGAN, 64 in this city, August 10th. Dr. Michael Regan a noted author and university professor was born in Newport on June 14, 1943. Educated at De La Salle Academy and Boston College, he received his doctorate from Georgetown. He was assigned to a post in the State Department shortly after graduation. A noted opponent of the Vietnam War, Dr. Regan resigned his diplomatic position after the Pentagon Papers were released by Daniel Ellsberg. In 1975 he published a scathing report criticizing the Nixon's administration's complicity in overthrowing Salvador Allende's government in Chile. Shortly thereafter, he left the United States to accept a position with a non-profit medical initiative in Argentina.

Regan spent the next three decades of his life working for change in Latin American politics, supporting democratic and occasionally socialist initiatives in Guatemala, Venezuela, Bolivia, Uruguay and Chile. He is the author of several works including *Unholy Capitalism* and *The New Left*. He has also co-authored several articles with Noam Chomsky of MIT. In 1992 he was appointed Regents Professor of Economics at the Universidad Privada de Santa Cruz, Bolivia. He is credited with proposing many of the domestic and regional policies which solidified Venezuelan and Bolivian alliances in recent years, including the regional bank founded by Venezuelan president Hugo Chávez. Dr. Regan was in Newport attending a conference at the Pell Center for International Relations. He is survived by his mother, Mary Conner Regan, a sister, Victoria Regan-Dalton, both of this city, and a son, Gary Regan, of Guadalajara, Mexico. A Latin requiem Mass will be held at St. Augustine's Church on August 15th, with burial at St. Colomba's Cemetery to follow. Friends and family are requested to send contributions to Doctors Without Borders in lieu of flowers.

"Any changes or suggestions?" Dr. Alioto asked.

"No, none. It looks fine. Thank you for doing this."

The intercom buzzed. "Governor Whitman to see you, sir."

"Let him in."

A vigorous man with a shock of gray hair, a trim moustache, and a well-tailored Italian herringbone suit entered the office. The ex-governor's smile was charming and embraced everyone there.

"Paul, good to see you! And Carolina, as beautiful as ever! And Gary, how long has it been? So, good to see *you.*" He shook Gary's hand and then clasped it even tighter with his other hand on top. Although only a lieutenant governor who finished out the term of his predecessor who died in office, everyone continued to use the honorific 'Governor' when they addressed him. Worth several hundred million dollars, the Governor was a descendant of the rich maritime traders who founded Newport. His influence in state and local politics was enormous. He clasped Gary's hand tighter.

"It's so sad that we meet again under these circumstances. I'm genuinely sorry for your loss."

Gary looked into his eyes and saw nothing but sincerity there. But sincerity was something seasoned politicians could fake. Still...

"Ah, I see you've been looking over the obituary. Do you think it does your father justice?"

"Yes, I do, Governor. Paul did a real good job."

"And is he taking care of you here? Providing you with the famed Newport hospitality?"

" Yes, he has been very generous. He's offered me a place to stay right on campus."

"Good. Take advantage. Relax; enjoy the place as much as you can under the circumstances. It is one of the loveliest settings in the world for a university. Anything we can do to make you comfortable, let Paul know. Also, I will be sending a limo for you to take you to the funeral. You're our guest."

"Thank you, sir."

"My pleasure, son. Now, there is one little thing you could do for me, Gary. Would you mind?"

"Anything, Governor."

"Ah, that's good. I was hoping you'd say that. I know that Carolina's husband had some unfounded suspicion that there might be foul play here. There was none of that, I assure you. Your father's death was an accident. But even the mere suggestion would really upset your grandmother. As a matter of fact, I almost went ahead and had your father's body cremated to save her from any more press interference in her life. She is an old and gracious lady and deserves peace and quiet in her retirement years, not parasitic reporters camped on her lawn. Don't you agree?

Yes, sir, but....

"No buts about it, Gary. Anyway, she objected to my cremation idea, so we'll go ahead with the funeral but it will be short and sweet. A traditional Catholic service, no smarmy memorial speeches, no visits from Chomsky or the Kennedys, or any other nonsense. And you and Carolina forget about all these foul play suspicions. Just not true."

"But...."

"I can assure you nothing untoward happened. I have the whole panoply of law enforcement at my disposal from my years in the governor's office. That includes the state police, the forensic folks, everybody. A simple, unfortunate accident. So, no digging around and muddying the waters, if you know what I mean."

"No, I'm not sure what you mean, Governor," countered Gary, not trying to conceal his growing annoyance.

"Well, if someone leaks to the papers that this case is not resolved, the reporters from New York and Providence will come flocking into town. Even CNN, for that matter! No one wants that, especially your grandmother and your Aunt Victoria. Your father caused a lot of heartache to your grandmother when he was alive. The scandal of the Pentagon Papers in which he was involved somehow, although never convicted. His accusations against Kissinger over the Allende assassination. And more recently his associations with Hugo Chávez in Venezuela. We don't need that kind of press attention and people digging into the past. This is a very conservative community and your Aunt Victoria depends on those kinds of people for her business."

"I see."

"I don't know if you do exactly. But I hope so, Gary." The Governor gripped the desk tightly and gave him an imperious stare. *He can be intimidating when he wants to*, Gary thought.

"When this is over, Gary, you'll go back to Mexico and your life there." He turned to Carolina and put his hand on her shoulder in a gesture of apparent solidarity. "The rest of us will have to stay and pick up the pieces. Isn't that right, Carolina? How is the good Lieutenant, by the way? Not home yet?"

It was smooth and casual. But Carolina felt the subtle threat there, the powerful influence which the last question suggested. The Governor could and would have people moved out of town, passed over for promotion, even demoted or fired if they interfered with his carefully orchestrated scenarios. He had done so in the past and would not hesitate to do so again.

CHAPTER NINE

It was after two by the time Dr. Alioto's graduate assistant delivered the bike and Gary settled into the second floor apartment of the Stoneacre building. It was more than adequate for his needs. There was a large living room well-appointed with a comfortable couch overlooking Ruggles Avenue and the tennis courts; an ample kitchen with all utensils and cooking supplies, and two simple but comfortable bedrooms furnished with bunk beds, writing desks, linen, blankets and towels. He convinced the security guard who gave him the keys to leave the fire door unlocked at the back of the apartment and to disable the alarm. This gave him access to the fire escape where he could sit outside in the evening and smoke a cigarette.

He made a quick trip with Carolina to the Stop and Shop on Bellevue to stock up on a week's worth of groceries and to also pick up an AA meeting list. When he settled into the apartment after thanking Carolina for her help and seeing her off, he made himself a corned beef sandwich on rye, opened a jar of spicy salsa and a bag of tortilla chips, and began to sketch out a plan. First, he would call his grandmother and set up a visit for tomorrow. Then he was going to ride the bike over to his Aunt Victoria's office on Memorial Boulevard. Later, after what he was sure would be an uncomfortable encounter, he'd hit an AA meeting. He noted on one of the campus message boards that there was an AA meeting right on campus just north of the administration building on Ochre Court.

His grandmother finally answered after a half dozen rings. She sounded a bit annoyed but agreed to meet with him the next day. She also told him that there would be no wake, since it was a closed casket because of the damage done by the salt water. The funeral would be on Saturday. A solemn requiem mass, but no dignitaries outside of the immediate family and a few representatives from the Pell Center. He didn't argue with her but kept it light, deferring to her feelings. It was, after all, her son who had died, and she had the right of the family matriarch to order things as she saw fit. Tomorrow would be soon enough for him to express whatever questions or reservations he had.

He called the real estate office of Regan and Stein and, once assured that his aunt was in, took the bike downstairs and set off. It had been a while since he had ridden a bike but it is something one never forgets. He turned right on Bellevue, pedaled up past Chateau sur Mar and stopped at the red light at Narragansett where he caught his breath. He pulled out as the signal changed and rode past De La Salle, the Elms, then the Tennis Hall of Fame and all the Bellevue boutiques. He turned right again on Memorial Boulevard and spotted the real estate office right around the corner, tucked in behind a coffee shop and up against the fence of the Casino tennis courts.

He walked into the reception area where multi-million dollar homes were displayed on easels like valuable canvases at the Louvre. No prices were listed, as if to say: *If you have to ask, you probably can't afford to buy*. He told the receptionist, an elegant and aloof young man in his early twenties, that he was there to see his Aunt Victoria. The young man looked him over, his eyes at first disdainful, then suspicious of Gary's tennis shorts and t-shirt. Finally, assuming that there was no accounting for taste, and that with so many indifferent-to-fashion wealthy people in town, it might be a mistake to bar him, escorted him back to Victoria's office.

"Gary," she said coming from behind her ornate Edwardian desk. "I heard you were in town. So, good to see you." Turning to her assistant, she said imperiously, "Thank you, Oliver, you can go."

Gary shook her hand; Victoria never hugged lest someone disturb her meticulously ironed blouse, or mash her expensively-coifed hairdo. Eighty- six years old but looking more like someone in her late fifties, it was clear that she stayed in shape. It was also clear that she had had a facelift or two to enhance the effect.

"Hello, Victoria. I'm sorry to bother you at work but I wanted to check out a few things with you before I went to visit grandmother."

"Have a seat, Gary. Coffee, tea, Perrier?

"No, thanks. I'm fine."

"So, what's on your mind? I'm sorry about your father's death. Of course, you two were never close, even less so in recent years. Still, there is always pain in the loss of a parent. Even if you don't feel it now, it will come when things have settled down. But my feeling is that you have something more specific in mind."

"Well, I was wondering a bit about the rush to get him in the ground and the lack of ceremony. The Governor explained some but it still seems to me a bit much. Also, from what I hear, his face was not that badly damaged, certainly nothing they couldn't fix at O'Neill's, yet Grandmother has ordered no wake and no open coffin. Finally, the police officer who investigated thought it might be more than a simple accident, but he was taken off the case and sent to Providence."

"Goodness," Victoria laughed brutally. "You make it sound like a conspiracy. You're a bit like your father in that. He was always seeing government and business conspiracies. His favorite lines were from Eisenhower's farewell speech in which he warned against 'the military industrial complex.' Yet, here we are enjoying this wonderful relationship between the Navy and the missile and aircraft industries which have brought so much prosperity to the region. Even the Internet, which you have to admit is the greatest achievement of your generation, is a product of the Defense Department and private industries. No, the conspiracies your father was so worried about never came to pass."

"But maybe there was a conspiracy he wasn't worried about, that caught him unawares," Gary offered.

Victoria frowned. "I doubt that very much. Certainly no one here would be involved. But there could have been something he was involved in down there in South America which came back to haunt him."

"But why would Grandmother be so secretive? Why would she try to get the Governor to close the investigation."

Annoyed, Victoria snapped, "Because of that damned Peter McGuire, that's why. He just wanted to dig up trash on the family. Why he even wanted the coroner to do DNA testing on Michael for no good reason that I could see. Said he wanted to make sure about the identification. At any rate, when you mother heard about that she called the Governor and asked him to get involved."

"But why should DNA testing disturb her? What difference would that make?"

Victoria blanched. "You'd have to ask your grandmother about her motivations. I'm sure I don't know. Now, Gary, if there's nothing else; it was lovely seeing you again, but I have work to do."

43

Gary got up, reached over and shook her hand. She did not offer her cheek to be kissed, so Gary simply turned and headed for the door.

"Oh, and Gary," she added, looking at his tennis shorts and t-shirt. "I hope you brought some decent clothes and a black suit. If not, please let Oliver know and he will make arrangements at Michael Hayes Clothing for you. We keep an account there."

"I'm fine, Victoria. I packed all I needed. And thank you. You've been very helpful."

When he exited the parking lot next to the realty office he observed the street person he had seen earlier. This time without the shopping cart. He did have something unusual, however. A large black plastic bag and, sticking halfway out of it, what appeared to be a surf fishing rod. *Unusual*, he thought. *Maybe the old guy goes surf fishing to keep himself fed. Although from what he thought he knew of street people, this was exceptional. Most, he felt, went for easier handouts or even dumpsters. Assuming this guy could even stay sober long enough to catch a fish, where could he clean and cook it?*

CHAPTER TEN

Tommy had seen the man on the bike before. Now, he remembered. *He was the fellow that Officer Rego had stopped on Bellevue earlier this morning. Hmm, someone new in town. But now he's riding a bicycle. Wonder if Rego impounded his car? Wouldn't put it past that son of a bitch.*

Tommy had had a fairly successful day. He had walked from Ruggles Avenue along the Cliff Walk, through the tunnel, past the Chinese tea house and out to Rough Point. Then, as he was headed back he saw something glint in a heavy patch of poison ivy beside the path. Since he used the protection of poison ivy to stash his bottles, knowing no one would ever reach in and grab one, he was intrigued. *Did someone else have the same idea?* He took out a small plastic shopping bag from his pocket, covered his hand carefully and then reached down into the bushes. The glint was from the brass fastenings on the cork base of a surf fishing rod. The butt of the rod was sticky with what felt like jam, or maybe sap from the poison ivy plants. He looked closer. *Perhaps blood?*

At any rate it was a decent enough pole. He did not think it was discarded there, but more likely stashed so that someone could pick it up later. He placed it carefully, stock-end first, in his black plastic trash bag and headed north toward First Beach. There were more people along this section of the Walk. Tourists, mostly. A group of Germans who were jabbering in their native tongue. Then a gaggle of Cub Scouts with their leader. To each of the groups he seemed invisible, and they barely stepped aside to let him go down the path.

When he got to the end of the Walk he rested and drank the last of his wine. He need to buy some more and was low on funds. He thought about going downhill to First Beach but decided that he'd had enough walking and scrounging for the morning. What he'd do now is head up Memorial Boulevard to Bellevue, and see if he could panhandle enough to get another jug of wine or--even better-- a pint of whiskey.

That was when he looked up he saw the guy on the bicycle weaving uncertainly out into the traffic, the same guy that Regan had stopped earlier in the day.

"Hey! It's one-way, buddy!"

Gary stopped when he heard the warning and straddled his bike. He looked over at Tommy and smiled. "Yeah, well, I'm only going up to the corner of Bellevue. I thought I could ride against traffic that far."

"You could," Tommy conceded. "But if Officer Rego sees you, he'll give you a ticket and probably impound your bike. In this town bikes have to follow the same rules as cars."

Gary got off the bicycle and walked along side Tommy. "Well, maybe you're right. I already ran into him once today."

"Is that what happened to your car? I saw you down by Narragansett this morning."

"Hey, that's right. I saw you, too. You had a shopping cart, right?"

"Tommy nodded and lit the stub of a discarded cigarette he had been saving from his walk. "Had to stash it. Officer Rego doesn't like to see shopping carts on his beat."

Gary took out his pack of Marlboro Lights and offered one to Tommy. "Here you go. Try one of these."

Tommy took two. One he put behind his ear and the other he lit up. They walked together up Memorial Boulevard and onto Bellevue. They turned left past La Forge restaurant, the Casino, the gallery of American art. When they got to the shopping center, Tommy made his proposal.

"Listen, you wouldn't have a couple of bucks you could spare so that I could get straight?"

Gary, an alcoholic in recovery, understood perfectly. He knew what it was like to go through withdrawals.

"Yeah, I can help you out. But listen. What do you have there, a surf fishing rod?"

"That's right."

"Is it for sale? Gary asked.

"Everything is for sale, my friend." Tommy described where he had found it, not far from Rough Point, stashed in poison ivy. He warned Gary not to grab the pole directly but only to hold it with the plastic bag covering the handle.

He drew it out of the trash bag. When he handed it to Gary, Gary could feel the plastic stick to the base. "What is the sticky stuff on the handle," he asked.

"Don't know. Could be jam or fish guts, maybe even blood," he laughed.

Gary suddenly grew serious. "And where did you find it again?" He remembered that Rough Point was where his father had gone over the cliff. He remembered, too, Lt. McGuire's speculation about the weapon. *Could this be it?*

"Look do you want it or not? Ten bucks."

"Sure, sure, I want it." Gary said, and he handed him the money.

While Tommy went to get his bottle of whiskey, Gary went into the Stop and Shop and bought some ice and Cokes, then met Tommy as he came out of the package store.

"Listen, If you've got nothing better to do, I'm new in town and could use the company. How about stopping at my place? You can drink in peace without Clementine Rego breathing down your neck, grab a shower if you want, watch a little TV."

"Clementine Rego, ha! I like that. Sure, how far from here do you live?"

Once inside the Stoneacre apartment, Tommy had a couple of shots to get straight and then took advantage of Gary's offer of a shower. Cleaned up and feeling almost human, he put some ice in two glasses and offered to pour Gary a drink.

"No, thanks, amigo. I gave up drinking a couple of years ago. Four years and three months to be exact."

"Yeah?" Tommy asked. "Why the fuck did you do that? It's one of the few real pleasures there are in life."

So, Gary told him his story. How alcohol simply stopped working for him. How it became an obsession which cost him his job and his dignity. And how at the end he wasn't even trying to get high, just stay normal and stop the shakes. Tommy drank some more and listened.

"I tried to get sober a couple of times, but it just didn't take," Tommy said. "Couldn't find anybody that I had anything in common with at them meetings. They were all high-bottom drunks."

After a while, Gary got up, turned on the TV and made them both bacon and scrambled eggs. As they sat watching a re-run of "The Sopranos," Tommy suddenly said, "I know who you are. You're Mike Regan's kid. Right? I knew your dad. A decent guy, always kind to me. He was another one never fit in here on this island."

"Do you know anything about how he died?"

"Heard he fell off the cliffs somewhere."

"That's right. Near Rough Point where you found the fishing rod."

"Jesus. You think, like, that could be his blood on the handle?"

"I don't know. I just know that it's worth checking out. Meanwhile I have to go to a meeting. It's not far from here and you can stay watch TV while I'm gone and finish your bottle."

"What kind of meeting?"

"An A.A. meeting. You don't have to go. Like I said, you can stay here. On the other hand, you're welcome to come with me if you want."

"Shit. All right, I don't mind tagging along. But they might kick me out if they think I been drinking."

"Well," Gary said thoughtfully, "you're not drunk yet. And the desire to stop drinking is all that's required. Just sit in the back with me, keep an open mind and listen. You might find this time around that you have more in common with those folks than you thought."

CHAPTER ELEVEN

"The AA meeting is at the Boat House, right down the road on the Salve Regina Campus. Do you know it?"

"Sure," Tommy said. "It's just back in the trees a bit, next to Angeles Hall. We walk down Ruggles, take a left on Ochre Point Ave and its just past the Admin Building."

"So, how are you feeling?"

"Okay. I feel even better knowing that I have half a fifth of whiskey to return to, just in case."

Gary wished that Tommy hadn't said that, but he knew the obsession with alcohol was as great as the insecurity of the person trying to leave it behind. For Tommy in his isolation, alcohol had become his only friend. And, if it sometimes turned against him, made him sick or got him into trouble, still…knowing it was always there when he needed it was a kind of security.

They found seats together in the back of the hall and Gary was pleased to see that it was a large group. Judging by their dress and conversations, they came from a broad range of social and economic backgrounds. There were lawyers there, retired teachers, but also fishermen, beach bums, teenagers, and landscapers. One woman had on a Chanel dress that probably cost $2,000, while another in an

Gary poured them both a drink of lemonade mix he had and put a bit of sugar in Tommy's to help with the urge. They went into the living room and sat down on the couch.

"Gary, I need to ask you for a big favor," Tommy said.

Oh-oh, here it comes, Gary thought. *He's going to hit on me for more money.*

"Well, if I can, Tommy. What is it?"

"I'd like you to be my sponsor."

Outside Gary heard the hoot of an owl and the rustlings of raccoons or maybe skunks in the brush. He opened the window wider and breathed in the fresh air. *Perhaps*, he thought, *I am not here to solve the mystery of my father's death. Perhaps I am here simply to help another human being recover his purpose in life.*

"I would be honored, Tommy," Gary replied. "Let's get through the night and we'll hit a meeting tomorrow morning." He handed him a small booklet that he had picked up at the meeting. "Here's the schedule. Let's just pick one out."

"How about this one in the basement of St. Joseph's Church? It's right across from the police station," Tommy asked.

How odd, Gary thought. *Why would he want to attend a meeting close to the police station?*

As if guessing what he was thinking, Tommy smiled. "It will give me a little boost if we run into Officer Rego when we're all together with our AA pals. Might make him step back a bit if he knows that we've got some friends in town, including a good lawyer."

CHAPTER TWELVE

Newport Hospital is located at Friendship Street and Broadway. Despite the rather corny sculpture at the entrance of an elderly person in a wheelchair assisted by a nurse, it is a world-renowned hospital. Only four percent of medical centers in the United States have been designated "magnet hospitals," Newport is one of them. None of that helped Gary's father who was beyond medical assistance by the time he arrived there. But Gary hoped that the hospital's high quality meant that the records of his father's death would be accessible and precise. A hospital like that could certainly not be part of a cover-up.

He had called earlier and set up a meeting with the emergency physician on duty at the time of his father's admittance, Dr. Tom Langford. He spotted the doctor when he saw the name tag on a thin, balding man in his mid-forties with a stethoscope around his neck catching a quick cigarette to the side of the hospital's covered entrance. Gary walked over and introduced himself.

"Ah, yes. You're the son of the accident victim on the cliffs."

Gary lit a cigarette as well. "Hi, doctor, yes. I'm Gary Regan. You were the attending physician?"

"Yes, that's right." He put out an elegant hand, smooth and with long, tapered fingers. Gary shook it firmly but carefully. "Pleased to meet you. My name is Tom Langford. I was on duty in the emergency room that night. I'm sorry for your loss."

"Could I maybe talk to the coroner? Is he around?"

Langford smiled. "We haven't had a coroner as such in a hundred years, Gary. That's a British term, as you know. And when we adopted that system in the American colonies, they were usually elected officials, not medical doctors, who determined the cause of death. Nowadays we have a state medical examiner system. But the primary reporter of a death is usually the attending physician who signs the death certificate."

"And in this case, that would be you?" Gary asked.

"That's correct. Finish your cigarette and then we'll go into my office and I'll go over my report and the death certificate."

"Could you tell me a bit more about the state medical examiner? Was he called in on this case? Was there an autopsy?"

"Well, the examining physician can call the state medical examiner based on his conclusions. If he does call, there are three responses available. Jurisdiction accepted. Jurisdiction accepted in absentia, meaning absent the body where the physician has submitted his report and sees no need of autopsy and the ME agrees. Finally, there is jurisdiction declined, which means there was no evidence of unexpected, unnatural or violent death."

"Well, the death here was certainly violent and unexpected."

"That's true. While there was no doubt in my mind about the cause of death, drowning, state law mandates that a forensic autopsy be performed when the cause is other than natural. So, notes from the homicide lieutenant at the scene, comments of the reporting officers, my external observation of the deceased, and diagnostic tests were sufficient for me to determine that the cause of death was accidental drowning due to a fall from a cliff. I faxed my report to the

Medical Examiner and he determined that a forensic autopsy was still necessary under state law. This, I should add, was contrary to the wishes of the family, heatedly expressed at the time. But I had no option."

"So, an autopsy *was* done over the objections of the family."

"Oh, yes indeed. And over the objections of the ex-governor as well," Dr. Langford added with a quick smile. "However, I don't think we learned much more from the autopsy than we had already known from my examination which was quite thorough. But come on inside, and we'll go over the notes."

The doctor's office was on the second floor. There were reports, folders and medical books on shelves, on his desk and even on the interview chair. Dr. Langford picked up a stack and put them on the floor so that Gary could sit.

"Okay, let's see. I will simply present you with the narrative. I wish to be respectful of your feelings here, Gary, so please tell me if you wish me to stop at any point. Sometimes this kind of narrative might seem raw and insensitive."

"I understand," Gary replied. "Please don't spare me, doctor. I just want to know the facts."

"Well, the subject was a healthy male with no visible scars or tattoos. Five feet, ten inches, one hundred and sixty pounds. According to documents found in his possession (U.S. Passport #3444566) he was sixty-four years of age at the time of death. Minimal body fat, normal muscular development for his age. The body presents some swelling of tissue consistent with immersion in sea water for an extended time. Traces of adipocere were found in both nostrils and the mouth...."

"What is that?" Gary asked.

"It's a kind of white froth," he explained. "It comes from the interaction of water with the soft tissues. To continue then, traces of adipocere were found in both nostrils and in the mouth which is consistent with death by drowning. Reverse: Fractured spine and two ribs. Pattern of lividity on the back. Crook of knees showing subcutaneous purple where they were bent against a rock on the beach."

"What is that?" Gary asked. "The purple color?"

"Kind of like a bruise, Gary, where the blood collects drawn by gravity. Shall I continue?"

Gary nodded.

"Okay, not much more. Flesh remained white where he'd been pressed against the surface of the beach. Also, the buttocks, shoulders and calves. So, hypostasis. He'd been lying dead in this position approximately 8-10 hours. The body had not been moved. The medical examiner opened the chest and the lungs were pale and distended, ballooning out of the cavity and the spaces between the ribs. All consistent with drowning. Toxicology screen was negative for drugs, alcohol or poisons.

"A more careful examination of the face revealed a slight abrasion of the skin over the left temple as well as a small two-centimeter contusion from a blunt force trauma. This was determined to have been minor and not sufficient to have caused either death or unconsciousness. Subject was alive and conscious when he hit the water as was determined from both the state of the lungs. Death by drowning due to accident. The certificate of death and the autopsy report are signed by both me and the state medical examiner."

"The contusion on the side of his head? That couldn't have killed him?

"No. It was minor. He might have just banged his head against a bit of floating debris as the body was carried to shore."

"What if someone hit him before he went into the water? Is that possible?"

"Well, anything is possible," Dr. Langford responded. "But he was conscious and alive when he went into the water. So, again, the blow was not the cause of death."

"Not the proximate cause," Gary said. "But might it have been a contributing cause. What if someone struck him, causing him to lose his balance and fall to his death?"

"We have no evidence whatsoever of that, Gary," Doctor Langford frowned.

"Not yet, you don't. But that doesn't mean such evidence doesn't exist. Tell me, Doctor. How can we get the medical examiner to re-open this case?"

CHAPTER THIRTEEN

The meeting the next morning at St. Joseph's was not until ten, so he called Carolina to find out if Pete McGuire would be back in the office before then. She told him that he had called from Providence earlier in the evening and expected to be back in his office by eight.

It would be a busy day. Drop off the fishing pole at the police station, and have Pete get someone at CSI to check it for blood and prints. He also needed to guide Tommy through his second AA meeting, and then meet his grandmother for lunch. His father's funeral was the following day and he had not yet had a moment to mourn or even to shed a tear.

They walked to St. Joseph's the following morning and, while Tommy attended the early mass to stay out of trouble and keep his mind off the drink, Gary went over to the police station on Broadway where he met Pete in the lobby and turned over the fishing rod.

"It might be nothing, but you did mention when we first discussed the case that something like this could have been a murder weapon."

"How did you come by it?" Gary asked holding it carefully so that the plastic bag did not smudge any evidence on the butt of the rod.

"It was found by a guy by the name of Tommy Murphy while he was scavenging along the Cliff Walk."

"You mean Tommy the Ragpicker? Jesus," Lt. McGuire observed shaking his head. "Not exactly what you'd call a reliable witness. And how did you persuade him to part with it?"

"I paid him. Ten bucks."

"Hmm. Well, you know you got a good deal. I'm a surf fisherman myself and I own tackle similar to this. These poles retail for about eighty-five dollars. Graphite stand-up rod, weighted cork handle with brass fitting. They're sold locally and should be easy to trace. Probably wouldn't have knocked the victim out but certainly would have given him the kind of bump I observed, and certainly would have knocked him off balance."

"So, what do you do now? Do you send it up to Providence to have someone check it out or what?"

"Well, some of that I can do myself. I was a CSI for ten years. I learned latent fingerprint processing and evidence collection at the Scientific Criminal Investigation School. The first thing we need to do is get you to write out a report so that we can establish chain of custody. I'll need Tommy to give me a statement, too. Then, I'll check for prints and then take it in person to the Rhode Island State Crime Laboratory and see if we can match the blood with the victim, and find any epithelials or other evidence that will give us a clue as to the assailant."

Gary was excited by the new development. Perhaps he was being of use after all. Maybe his father's death would be resolved. "What happens after that?"

"Well, then we'll see if we can convince the medical examiner to re-open the case and treat this as a homicide."

They went into his office and Gary wrote out a statement explaining how he came by the evidence. He offered to take a statement from Tommy himself, because he knew that Tommy would be nervous about coming over to the police station. He explained to Gary about Tommy's new sobriety and how fragile that was.

"Okay, have him describe exactly where it was that he found it. If you can get him to actually walk with you to the spot, that would be very helpful. I can go out there using that description and take some measurements and integrate it into my crime scene notes. It looks like we're actually moving on this. Good work, Gary. You've accomplished a lot more than I expected. Come on, I'll walk you outside. Where are you headed next?"

They passed the front desk and cleared the security walkthrough. The lieutenant nodded to the information officer as they walked by.

"I have an AA meeting with Tommy over at St. Joseph's. Then, I'm meeting my grandmother for lunch at her house."

"She'll probably tell you to back off. She'll try to convince you to go the funeral, be a good boy, and then get on the next flight to Mexico. And be prepared for her to tell you not to trust me as well."

"Why should she tell me that?" Gary asked.

"It's a long story. Remember I told you that I was a CSI for ten years? Well, after that I was on patrol for another decade—kind of a demotion because I stepped on a few people's toes. Then I was transferred to the Property Office. I took care of evidence, essentially. Anyway, I had a hard time making lieutenant. I was passed over eight times by candidates who ranked lower than me on the lieutenant's exam. When I asked the Chief for the reasons, I was given the same boilerplate answer each time. Finally, with the help of the union I took it to arbitration. The arbitrator ruled that the Chief had violated my contract by not providing me with reasons for passing me over. She gave him a chance to do so at the hearing but he declined. So, she ruled in my favor. I was promoted to lieutenant with back pay, seniority, and all benefits back to five years. It made several people pretty angry.

"Well, I later found out that one of the reasons I had been passed over was from political pressure. I had dug up some information on a cold case that involved a wealthy heiress by the name of Doris Duke, who had formed a foundation that provided millions for a home restoration project which was giving jobs to a lot of Newporters. Your grandmother and the Governor both were on the Foundation's committee."

"So, what happened?"

"We both won, more or less. The Foundation's project went through and was very successful. Your grandmother made some money there, I believe. A couple of her relatives lease houses that were part of the project. The Governor and his son got very good publicity. The charges against Doris Duke were not pursued. As a matter of fact the Chief actually took retirement four months after he closed off the investigation. I got tired of pursuing the case and, with a career that was going nowhere, Carolina and I fighting all the time over money…. Well, I'm ashamed to say that by the time I finally got the union to take my case to arbitration, I had tanked my investigation."

"What did the cold case involve? Murder?"

"Yep. You can research it if you want. The victim was Eduardo Tirella. The case was back in 1966. You'll find plenty of files in the library. It certainly was a low point for Newport's Finest. But then there's a tradition of the rich getting away with murder, isn't there? That's part of what motivated your father to do the work he did."

Gary hadn't thought of his father in that way. He tended to picture him as an academic. But he supposed what Pete said was true. His work in Latin America was certainly part of unraveling a system that he led to the wholesale exploitation and disenfranchisement of the poor at the hands of a small group of rich landowners, generals, and multi-national corporations.

CHAPTER FOURTEEN

Gary rode his bike across Bellevue and down Ruggles enjoying the rush of the wind as he coasted down the hill, and then the tightness in his thighs as he pumped up to Carroll Avenue. He peddled past the tennis courts and the granite slide at Murphy Field, crossed Old Fort Road and went up to Harrison. At noon the August sun was bright and the humidity had risen along with the temperature so he was relieved as he crossed the street and pulled into the shade of his grandmother's property.

His grandmother's house was a comfortable cottage built at the end of the Second World War for less than $20,000. Now, the three-bedroom home was worth half a million. The front yard was surrounded by a low privet hedge, while carefully pruned azaleas and blue hydrangeas lined each side of the walkway. Gary thought of the blue hydrangea as the distinctive Newport blossom. You saw it everywhere: in the gardens of the rich and famous, in the public parks, and beside the small cottages of the middle class merchants and professionals who formed the core of the island's economy. His grandmother's flowerbeds were planted in fuchsia and chrysan-themums, snapdragons and petunias, with sweet alyssum bordering the walkway. Her neat cottage was white, newly painted, with black trim. In Newport because of the sea mist, wooden houses showed their wear if they were not painted every four years, his grandmother had not neglected hers and it shone in the morning light.

He knocked at the front door and his grandmother, who was waiting on the sun porch for his arrival, opened the door to greet him. Mary Conner Regan was a thin woman who bore her ninety years with casual grace. Slightly bent with arthritis and leaning into an aluminum walker, she nevertheless tilted her head graciously to receive his kiss like the family matriarch she was. Her hair was carefully dressed in a tight cap of gray curls; her eyes were bright and intelligent.

"Gary!" she smiled. "It is *so* good to see you. I heard you were in town and I was wondering if you'd ever come by to see me."

"I'm sorry, Grandma," he said, bending down to kiss her proffered cheek. "I've been doing quite a bit of running around."

"So I heard from the Governor," she said dryly. "Well, come in, come in. Let's go into the kitchen; that's still where real people meet in my house. Nothing fancy. We'll be having iced tea, ham sandwiches and fresh fruit.

At the kitchen table was a short dark haired woman who had set an iced tea pitcher on the table and was efficiently arranging the napkins and silverware."

"This is Pilar," his grandmother introduced them. "She comes by every day to help out for a few hours. Pilar, this is my grandson Gary, from Mexico. Pilar is from Guatemala."

"*Buenas tardes, Señor Gary. Como estâ?*

"*Muy bien, Pilar. Y tú?*"

"*Bien también, Señor. Trabajar para su abuela es un gran honor. Su abuela habla de usted todo el tiempo. Me dijo que usted es tenista muy famoso.*"

"*Fui,*" Gary smiled. "*En el pasado. Ahorita, soy un entrenador humilde.*"

"Okay, thank you, Pilar," his grandmother interrupted impatiently. "I think we're all set up here. I know you have another home to visit. So you can go. Do you need me to pay you something now or can you wait until Friday?"

"Friday *está bien, Señora*. Then turning to Gary, "*Tengo mucho gusto en conocerle.*"

"*El gusto es mío*," Gary smiled and gave her a gracious bow as she passed and headed out the door.

When Pilar left, his grandmother sat down heavily in the kitchen chair and instructed Gary to pour the tea. He served them each a sandwich and some tortilla chips from a bowl. After they had each taken a sip of the iced tea she began to question him.

"So, what's this I hear about you working as a junior G-man, investigating your father's accident?"

"Well, that's just it. We're not entirely sure it was an accident. Lieutenant McGuire seemed to think that there was a bit of a rush to get the whole thing swept under the rug. Someone tried to convince the attending physician not to order an autopsy. There was even a suggestion that Dad's body was to be cremated."

Gary looked closely to see how she'd react to this. He expected that she would be upset, especially if she did not have a hand in the orders. Instead she simply set her lips in an annoyed grimace. She took a bite out of her sandwich, chewed it slowly and then spoke.

"Well, well. You've been doing your homework I see. But this Johnny-come-lately police lieutenant you seem to put so much stock in is a busybody type. Seems to have a lot of time on his hands as well. He's fascinated by celebrities and likes to create a bit of notoriety for himself. So, you might want to spend some of your investigative talent checking out his background."

"I take it you're referring to his trying to re-open the Doris Duke case?"

"Oh, you heard about that, did you? Well, it doesn't stop there, I'm afraid. Alan Dershowitz had to get an injunction against him in the Von Bulow case. It seems that he went after that poor man even after the courts had ruled Klaus should be left alone.

"I thought Von Bulow was convicted of killing his wife?"

"The conviction was reversed by the courts when Alan... you've heard of Alan Dershowitz?

"Wasn't he the law professor from Harvard who wrote the book about the religious right hijacking the Constitution?"

"Actually hijacking the Declaration of Independence, if I'm not mistaken. In this case it was local law enforcement and prosecutors who were hijacking the Constitution. Anyway, he pointed out the glaring errors that the police and the prosecution made in the case, and the appeals court quickly reversed. It never should have gone to trial. But that didn't stop your vicious friend McGuire from hounding poor Klaus until Alan got a court order for him to desist."

"Well, that may well be, Grandma. But it does seem that there are some issues...."

"And why would McGuire involve you in the first place? Did you ask yourself that? I think if you check you'll find that he was passed over for promotion on several occasions. He sees this as an opportunity to grab some media attention in the hopes that it will promote his career and he's using you to do his dirty work. Annoying little man! He fancies himself to be one of those CSIs like they have on TV."

"But someone did try to close down the investigation. Isn't that true? Was it the Governor?"

"No, it was me. I didn't want any scandal to be associated with your father's death. That's all there was to it. Nothing could be gained by bringing up the past, or by trying to find a crime where none existed. My feeling was that once that kind of thing started, there would be no end to it and lives would be ruined unnecessarily."

"I don't know what you mean," Gary said puzzled. "Whose lives would be ruined?"

"Well, it's a long story. So let's have a bit of this fruit and sit back." She served them both a portion of blueberries, sliced apple and melon. "Some of the things I'm going to tell you will be a bit of a shock," she began. "But I'm too old to apologize. What's done is done.

"It began back when I was a young girl. My father was the head gardener for the Vanderbilts. He was an Irish immigrant, very smart and gifted. He was one of the founders of the Professional Gardeners Association and he often went to other estates to consult with less experienced gardeners on plantings. He was a noted horticulturalist as well and was in demand by everybody from flower show fanciers to landscape architects like Jacques Graber and Frederick Law Olmsted, who designed Central Park in New York. I used to accompany him on his visits during summer vacations and sometimes I would play with the children of the estate owners while he went about his work. Occasionally, I was even invited to their parties. I was a charming child, attractive and well-spoken. Several times I even played a bit of lawn tennis (maybe that's where you got your talent from) with some of the young people. One summer, when I was sixteen, I went out on a sailing party with a group of young rich boys and their dates.

"My father knew nothing of this adventure. We all lived in a more innocent age then, and he thought me incapable of deceiving him. Anyway, one of the boys brought some brandy and we drank a bit, and that evening I went *all the way,* as we used to say, with a handsome young man. I think I probably seduced him, rather than the other way around. As I remember he was quite shy. At any rate, I thought I was in love and I believe he was, too. I was only sixteen, as I said, and he was eighteen. The boy's name was Clayton Whitman, the son of a wealthy and influential family. Marriage was out of the question. If my father were to even suggest such an accommodation, the Whitmans would have seen that he lost his job; they would insure that he would never work on any estate in Newport, or on the East Coast for that matter. I would be labeled a tramp, and my family would never live down the scandal. You see, to people like the Whitmans we were disposable people.

"The Whitmans' first proposal to pay for an abortion was rejected by my mother and father out of hand. They were both practicing Catholics and very strongly opposed to that. Then a second offer was made. The Whitman family would raise the child as their own; give it a good education as well as their family name. So, it was agreed. I was sent off to a secret location at one of the Whitman properties in New Hampshire.

"When I came to term I gave birth to non-identical twins—both boys. The first boy went to the Whitmans, as agreed. The second child I kept, and later Whitman allowed one of the estate workers, a good Catholic boy who had a crush on me, to marry me. That was your grandfather William, and I will be forever grateful to him."

"So, my father's brother, my uncle is…."

"Yes, Parker Whitman, who is on the short list for the position of Supreme Court justice. So you see, both I and the governor, your *real* grandfather by the way, have a vested interest in seeing this case closed quickly. It cannot benefit anybody to have the investigation go on. Your father is dead. You need to grieve for him, remember the good things he's done, and then get on with your life. This probing and searching of yours won't bring him back, and will only cause others pain."

"Just tell me the rest of the story," Gary snapped.

"Don't take that self-righteous tone with me, Gary. You of all people. Haven't you learned anything in those twelve step meetings of yours about tolerance and forgiveness?"

"I'm sorry, Grandmother," Gary replied, a bit ashamed that he was in fact taking the old lady's inventory.

"As you should be. Well, there's not much more to tell. I returned home to Newport fourteen years later. I was homesick and wanted to settle back in my hometown. In exchange for a promise to keep the secret of Michael's birth, we were given a significant monthly check from the Whitmans and the promise that Michael's education would be paid. I enrolled Michael at De La Salle Academy where he was an Honor Roll student for all four years. William and I bought this beautiful house for cash which the Whitmans supplied. The price was my silence. Michael went on to Boston College and graduated Phi Beta Kappa. He did his graduate studies in economics and Latin American Studies at Georgetown. The Governor did *so* want to be proud of him.

"Unfortunately, Michael was a rebel from an early age. He rejected the conservative values of William and me, marching in Alabama with Negroes for civil rights, protesting the war in Viet Nam, and god knows what else. He was involved in dozens of protests and demonstrations and finally arrested in New Hampshire for blocking the construction of a nuclear plant at Seabrook. Gov. Whitman used his influence to get him released from jail, his record expunged, and an assignment as a minor functionary with the State

Department based on his language skills and his background in economics.

"Then he was assigned to the State Department where he leaked documents causing embarrassment to our government, and especially to Secretary Kissinger, by revealing America's complicity in the overthrow of the Allende regime. Your father seemed determined to reject the values and philosophies of those who helped him. He was anti-capitalist, anti-imperialist and soon found himself in bed with the leftist factions in South America. After being fired by the State Department, he worked as a free-lance economist advising governments in Nicaragua, Venezuela, Bolivia and even Uruguay on how to formulate successful socialist policies.

"He was in the press quite a bit recently, along with this fellow Chomsky, the MIT radical, who also seems to reject every policy the U.S. puts forth. He seems to think that Hugo Chávez is the reincarnation of Franklin Roosevelt, even though the rest of us see him as the next Fidel Castro. So your father's coming to the Pell Institute for this globalization conference was just another thorn in the Governor's side. But what's done is done. Michael is gone. I grieve for him, but it was an accident and no good can come from raking over the coals of his passing.

"You need to let sleeping dogs lay, Gary. You need to go back home after the funeral tomorrow, return to your wife in Mexico. Newport is not a place for you. It was a not a place for your father, and there is even less here for you than there was for him."

Gary shook his head. Whether in disagreement, confusion, or just refusal to take in all that had been said, he didn't know. He just found that he could not agree with her at any level right now.

"So you told me about my father. Tell me about your other son. What happened to my Uncle Parker, the boy adopted by the Whitmans?

"Well, he went to St. George's Prep, then to Harvard, then to a career as an attorney in Boston. He is also the heir to a fortune of more than $60 million. But more to the point is the Governor's son, born three years later. Clayton Whitman III is a state senator and a fool. Something of a braggart, involved in petty political shenanigans. Of course, he's managed to piggy-back on his father's name to have some influence in Providence, but overall he's been a disappointment. Gambling, even problems with organized criminals. He's another of the reasons we can't afford this scandal. He's always been jealous of your Uncle Parker and this would give him just the ammunition he needs to destroy Parker's chances with the Supreme Court. Do you have any other questions?"

"No, Grandma, it will take a while just to absorb all this."

"Well, there is one more question you might want to ask of your friend Detective McGuire."

"What's that?"

"Just how close is he to Clayton William III and whose side will he be on when the chips begin to fly."

CHAPTER FIFTEEN

After checking in with Tommy and making sure he was still sober and relatively tranquil, Gary headed to the Newport Public Library in the shady park off Spring Street. He loved visiting this library. Although it had moved to a newer building in Acquidneck Park, it was even better organized than he remembered and had an experienced staff that was friendly and helpful. He did a computer search for Doris Duke and then skimmed through the many documents to find the incident that both McGuire and his grandmother had referred to. Between the news stories in the *Providence Journal* and the investigative reporting of the *New York Times* he was able to piece together the narrative.

Doris Duke, the "richest girl in the world," as she was known to the *Times* reporter, inherited a vast fortune at age twelve when her father James Buchanan Duke died. Her father was the founder of a tobacco cartel responsible for the sales of 80% of all tobacco products in the U.S. As a result of the trust busting of Teddy Roosevelt, he was forced to scale back his activities, but the American Tobacco Company was, nevertheless, a major player well into the 20th century. Her father's death by pneumonia was probably accelerated by his wife leaving all the windows open (it was autumn) in their bedroom during his illness while she sat bundled up by his side and watched him slowly die.

At his death, Doris inherited a number of mansions, farms and other properties. She sued her mother at the age of 14 to stop her from selling off property left by the estate. She won that suit and at an early age, with the help of talented legal and fiscal advisers, had taken full control of the empire left to her. One of her favorite homes was in Newport, Rhode Island, which she neglected after the Hurricane of 1938 but ultimately, after her mother's death, began to prefer over all the others. She began to refurnish it with valuable art and antiques throughout the Sixties; she lived in luxury there from May through November each year while spending the winters in Hawaii. She lived a rather wild life, indulged in various drugs including LSD and cocaine. She drank heavily as well.

On October 7, 1966 as she was leaving her ten-acre Bellevue Avenue estate in the company of Eduardo Tirella, her interior decorator, something happened that has forever blackened the annals of Newport history.

They proceeded down the elegant driveway to the front entrance headed for Bellevue Avenue. At the end of the driveway, Tirella stopped the car to open the massive iron gates which guarded the property. The gates were chained and padlocked. While Tirella was in the process of unlocking them, Duke slid over to drive the car through. She then gunned the car, a new Chrysler station wagon, which slammed Tirella against the gates, and dragged his body across the avenue where the car was finally stopped by a tree. Tirella was pronounced dead at the scene from massive head trauma.

Ms. Duke was taken to the hospital for treatment of minor facial cuts and shock. She was released without any drug screen or alcohol testing. Amazingly, Newport Police never formally questioned Duke about the matter until several days later, when her well-paid New York attorney was present. Duke at first denied that she was driving the car. Then she admitted she was driving but said that when the car started to go forward she put her foot on the gas instead of the brake. She said that the car had a new automatic (push button) transmission that she was not used to because she had driven it on only one prior occasion.

The police announced after the interview that they had no reason to believe it was anything other than a freak accident. Duke herself continued to blame the car. The press suggested a cover-up. Tirella's family sued. Not only locals but most newspaper readers of the day were outraged at what seemed to by a blatant abuse of justice. The Newport Police Chief took early retirement. No criminal charges were ever filed. But some other interesting things did happen in the months which followed.

First, Doris Duke launched the Newport Restoration Foundation and provided it with a multi-million dollar grant to preserve the historic houses in Newport which were woefully neglected and had become eyesores. She managed to convince Jacqueline Kennedy of nearby Hammersmith Farm to be the first vice-president, and thereby ingratiated herself with the local movers and shakers and resumed her place of respect in high society. She also gave a large cash settlement to Tirella's family, thus choking off any civil suits.

But most interesting of all to Gary was the next bequest, not mentioned in the *Times* article, but receiving some prominence in the *Newport Daily News* as well as the *Providence Journal.* Doris had objected for years to people hiking along the Cliff Walk, and disputed the right-of-way which had authorized citizens to pass along the sea cliffs for hundreds of years. In fact, she blocked off sections of the Cliff

Walk with boulders, chain link fences, and even allowed aggressive dogs to run loose on the property all the way to the sea cliffs to discourage anyone passing by. After the death of Tirella, she suddenly changed her mind. She not only removed the boulders, fences and dogs but she contributed a significant sum for the development of the Cliff Walk Restoration Project, endearing herself to the locals.

He remembered what his grandmother had said about how the Whitmans considered her father and mother "disposable people." He thought that Doris Duke probably shared the same world view. The people of her class and status were the ones that really counted in the world. The rest existed only to serve them. In her mind, this servant class included not only maids, butlers and gardeners but also senators and governors, police chiefs and attorneys-general. The Dukes, like plutocrats in banana republics bought and sold justice on the island and disposed of people as thoughtlessly as if they were soiled linen.

Gary was about to end his search when something caught his eye. The name of the estate where Doris Duke had the accident. The English manor with thirty-seven rooms and ten acres of land. It was called "Rough Point," and that, he remembered, was where his father had gone over into the sea, where the body had been found.

He went to a pay phone and called Tommy.

"How're you doing, Tommy? Still hanging in there okay?"

"Yep. I drank most of your lemonade though, and ate a bunch of that hard candy. Can't seem to get enough of it. Also, I been reading that "Big Book" you left me but I find it hard to concentrate. Mostly, I've been watching TV."

"No problem. Listen, try to eat some fruit; there's peaches and plums in the refrigerator. Fructose is a better kind of sugar for people in early alcohol withdrawal. You don't get the rush and then depression that come from regular sugar. Try it, okay? And, listen, about dinner.... I was thinking of picking up some corn and some lobsters. How does steamed lobster and corn on the cob sound to you? Then we'll hit the eight-thirty meeting at the Boat House."

"Sounds great, Gary! Thanks."

"Listen, one other thing. The place where you found the fishing pole...do you think if we walked the Cliff Walk tomorrow you could take me there? I mean, do you remember where it was?"

"Sure. I remember the exact place. I can take you there. It's just this side of the old Doris Duke estate where an old *rosa rugosa* hedge grows wild and there are waist high patches of poison ivy. It's a pretty tricky place to walk. As a matter of fact it's called...."

"Don't tell me. Let me guess. It's called "Rough Point.""

CHAPTER SIXTEEN

Gary rode his bike down to Bannister's Wharf where he found a small fishing boat off-loading lobsters. He hailed the owner of the skiff, a gray-haired Portuguese fisherman with a barrel chest and a dark tan.

"Got any culls for sale?" he called out.

The man looked him over. Selling directly from a boat was illegal, since it avoided state and local taxes, and also inspections by Fish and Game who were concerned about indiscriminate trapping of young, undersized shellfish. Apparently satisfied that Gary was no threat, he held up two small lobsters: one missing a claw, the other seemingly intact.

"I can let you have these. Eight bucks each. They go about a pound and a half apiece."

Since the going rate for fresh lobster was about twelve dollars a pound, it was a good deal. Gary gave him the cash and the lobsterman dropped them in a double-thick freezer bag and handed them up to the dock.

When he arrived home he greeted Tommy with a warm hug, assuring himself from the lack of alcohol odor that Tommy was still holding up his end of the sobriety agreement. He boiled water for the lobsters, instructed Tommy to shuck the corn, and melted two sticks of butter in a small pan. While the lobster boiled, he prepared a light salad, poured two glasses of iced tea, and sliced half a loaf of French bread. When they sat down to dinner, Tommy told him about his day, which included cleaning up the kitchen and bathroom and vacuuming the living room. Gary was impressed.

"Oh, and you got a call from the cop, McGuire. I told him about where I found the surf fishing rig and he asked me about signing something. I told him, no problem, that I'd do it. He also said for you to call him back. You also got a call from your wife. She said she's in Bolivia and everything is okay. She's going out to some dinner tonight with the university people but will try calling back in the morning.

When they finished their meal, Gary set up a pot of espresso coffee and then called McGuire while the steaming water was dripping through the filter.

"What's up, Pete?"

"I talked to your guest. Sounds like he's staying sober."

"Yeah, he's hanging in there," Gary said.

"Good going. I hope it works out. He's really a decent guy when he's sober. Real smart, too. Used to teach biology at Rogers High years ago until the booze got him. He was something of an expert on the local flora. Lots of folks remember his field trips from when they were kids.

"Anyway, the reason I called is that I had the Crime Lab run the fishing pole for prints, epithelials and blood. We came up positive for blood. Human, B positive. Same type as the victim...damn, I mean your Dad. Also, we got a partial print which we ran through CODIS and NCIC. But no hits. Then I decided to send them over to ICE, the Homeland Security version of INS enforcement these days, and I got a positive. Seems like they belong to a Central American immigrant, one Juan Miguel Andrade, nineteen years old, a Guatemalan refugee. He's only been in the country a couple of months. He was initially here illegally, came up through Mexico. But he managed to get a deportation hearing in federal district court in Providence and was granted asylum. So now he's as legal as they come. Driver's license and everything," McGuire paused as if deciding how much more of the investigation he should reveal to a civilian.

"Anything else?" Gary prodded.

"Yeah, it seems like he had a relative in Newport, so he moved down here. I got the address and sent a patrol there. I spoke to his cousin, one Pilar Andrade and she said that she hadn't seen Juan Miguel for two days. Anyway, we have a warrant out for his arrest."

"What was the name of the cousin again?" Gary asked.

"Pilar Andrade. Why? Does it ring any bells?

"Did you ask her what she did for a living?"

"Yes, she works part-time as a house cleaner for several families."

"I think my grandmother is one of the people she works for. In fact," Gary added quite certain now. "I think I met her today."

"Shit. Well, I don't want to deal with your grandmother any more than I have to. She probably wouldn't give me a straight answer anyway. Why don't you see if you can follow up on that? Anyway, it's a small island and we should find him if he's still in town. I have a statewide alert out for him."

"Okay," Gary agreed. "I can do that. Let me suggest something else, Pete. I have a friend in El Salvador who tried to get asylum a few years back. It was a pretty Byzantine process. Why don't you see if you can find out who sponsored him in the U.S.? Having a relative and a place to stay might be helpful, but he would have needed a respectable citizen to speak up for him at the hearing and he would have needed a job. I don't think any federal judge would just let him waltz into Newport with nothing."

"Good idea. I'll check on that, too, and get back to you. Say…tomorrow's the funeral, right?"

"Yeah, at St. Augustine's," Gary confirmed.

"Okay, well, I'll see you there." Pete paused for a second. "Or, better yet, How about meeting for breakfast at the Ocean Breeze? It's down there in the Fifth Ward just the other side of Wellington Avenue. Supposed to be the best breakfast in town and you'll need your strength if you're going to hit the funeral, the interment out at St. Colomba's, and also do some follow-up questioning."

"Sounds like a deal, Pete. I'll see you there at eight. The funeral's at nine."

"Say, Gary, one more thing. You wouldn't know of any reason why a Guatemalan would have it in for your father, would you?"

"No. My Dad hadn't been active in Central America since the Eighties. Most of his recent work was in Venezuela and Bolivia."

Gary hung up and joined Tommy in the kitchen where he had begun washing the dinner dishes and pots. Gary helped him finish up, dried the dishes and put them away. They each poured their coffee, and then went out into the living room. Gary explained about the statement he needed from Tommy for the police, then he drafted a one-page affidavit stating how Tommy had come to find the fishing pole, where he had taken it, and how it came into Gary's custody. Gary explained that it was necessary to prove chain of custody. After reading it over, Tommy signed it and Gary added his own signature as witness.

"Lieutenant McGuire believes that it was the weapon that caused my father's death."

Tommy squeezed his arm in sympathy. "Don't worry, Gary. They'll get the guy. McGuire is a persistent son-of-a-bitch. Most of the other cops don't like him because he's a bulldog and doesn't always play by the rules. But I think he's a good man."

They re-filled their coffee cups and went out the security door which had been disarmed and sat on the fire escape. They both lit up cigarettes.

"Tonight will be an important meeting for you, Tommy."

"Why's that?"

"Because you'll get your first chip. Twenty-four hours of sobriety."

"Shit. Twenty-four hours is nothing. I want ninety days; then I'll feel like I accomplished something."

"Whether it's ninety days, or four and a half years like I have, Tommy, it's still one day at a time. Just stay sober for the next twenty-four hours and it will add up."

They sat for a while looking up at the stars, each in his own separate world, enjoying the peace of the moment, the silence, the soft wind in the trees. Gary said a small prayer of gratitude, a habit that he had cultivated in early sobriety but that he had neglected recently. Then the phone rang and he went inside to answer it.

"Gary, this is Paul Alioto over at the Pell Center. I just called to see how everything is and how you're settling in."

"Fine, just fine, Paul. Thanks for calling."

"I'm told that you have a guest there."

"Yes," Gary paused. He thought about saying more and then remembered the AA tradition of anonymity. "Yes, a friend."

"I see," said Alioto as if hoping for more. "Well, um...you're certainly welcome to have a guest, of course. Just let Security know so that they'll have him on their list. They have instructions to stop outsiders from going into the building or even being on the grounds for that matter, if they're not registered."

"Okay. I'll take care of that."

"Listen, the real reason I'm calling is that I want you to know that we'll all be at the funeral. Despite some differences of political opinion, everyone respected and admired your Dad."

"Thanks, Paul," Gary was suddenly touched. "I appreciate that."

"The second thing is that I ran into a brigadier general from Bolivia today. He's attending a conference at the Naval War College. Something about hemispheric security issues."

"How strange. A *Bolivian* general?"

"Yes, I know that sounds odd but the Naval War College often hosts commanders from the armed forces of other allied countries with the intention of bringing them up to speed on issues of mutual security. Anyway, I told him about the accident and he expressed his deep regrets. Actually, it was a bit more than that. When I told him about your father's death he seemed quite upset. It seems he knew your father and had hoped to speak with him at our conference. So, I told him that you were here and he said that he'd like to meet with you. He'll be at the funeral. Perhaps you can speak to him then?"

"Fine. Introduce us after the funeral and I'll find a time for us to talk," Gary said.

"Good. Then I'll let you go. Oh, and don't forget to register your friend at Security if he's spending another night. And speaking of guests... you are certainly welcome to invite your wife to join you here, if you intend staying for a while.

"Thanks for that, Paul. She's in Bolivia right now as a matter of fact, wrapping up my father's affairs. I expect to hear back from her some time tomorrow."

"Really? In Bolivia? Well, that's good, I suppose. Divide the labor. Well, listen, when this is all over, I was hoping we could get together and play a little tennis. Maybe I could pick your brain about Mexico. I'm always interested in the perspective of people who have actually lived abroad. So many of our experts only make short visits to the countries they write about and spend most of their time in academic circles. Despite their authoritative stances in their books and position papers, they often have only a superficial knowledge."

"Well, I'm no expert in anything but I'll be glad to share my impressions."

When they hung up Gary thought that perhaps that was the biggest problem with American society. This reliance on self-styled experts and pseudo-professionals, and no ordinary citizen trusting himself or herself to know what the reality was. Unless you had a degree, a credential, a badge, or a position of some kind, no one took your opinion seriously. In fact, most people had gotten out of the habit of thinking for themselves, so that is was fairly easy for Homeland Security, the Attorney General and the Justice Department to deprive them of their rights and constitutional protections as citizens, as their elected Congressmen sat idly by. Nowadays, "American citizen" was a meaningless designation. It did not even earn you common courtesy in airports and train terminals. How odd. Especially when you thought about 9/11 and how the only plane which had been stopped was due to the unified effort of ordinary American citizens. They saw what needed to be done. They organized, planned, and then acted in concert, destroying the plane and the hijackers.

Meanwhile, in New York, the FAA and the Air Force delayed in typical bureaucratic befuddlement until it was too late and those planes crashed into the towers, killing thousands. And in

Washington, the nation's capital, the military and federal authorities were more concerned with getting Bush and his staff into hiding than protecting private citizens or even their own employees at the Pentagon. The only successful battle against terrorism was fought in the air over Pennsylvania by ordinary Americans. Everyone seemed to forget that. And the government appeared to be intent these days on emasculating the citizens who are the country's only real defense.

Well, he and Tommy were two free citizens. They hadn't done much with that up to now. Maybe it was time for a change. Maybe an ordinary citizen could change the way things were.

CHAPTER SEVENTEEN

Saint Augustine's Church does not appear on any of the tourist maps of Newport. It is not as famous as St. Mary's where President Kennedy married Jacqueline Bouvier, nor as culturally relevant as St. Joseph's which has opened its doors to the new immigrant population and offers a Mass in Spanish. Tucked away behind high privet hedges on the corner of Harrison and Carroll avenues, it is a church that time has passed by. The cement walkway is cracked and the lawn is casually trimmed. To the left of the entrance on a pedestal rests a rather rudimentary sculpture of St. Augustine, the renowned Bishop of Hippo and author of *The City of God*. The piece was crafted by Felix DeWeldon who created the famous sculpture of the Marines raising the flag over Iwo Jima, a work much more accomplished than this inelegant statue he chipped out for the poor Irish Catholics at a bargain rate.

For years St. Augustine's was the parish church for the maids, cooks, gardeners and coachmen who staffed the great estates of the barons of the Gilded Age. Their children became the bartenders, teachers, restaurateurs and police of the city. Now that the dynamics of the global economy have changed and estate taxes have made ownership of large acreage and houses staffed with many servants untenable, the grandchildren of those original immigrants have gone off to New York, Los Angeles and Chicago to seek their fortunes. The ageing population left behind in the parish these days consists of retirees on fixed incomes and a handful of city employees. The church has assumed a seedy aspect, and the number of parishioners at daily mass has dwindled to a handful of neighborhood ladies too old to walk more than a few blocks.

During the weekdays the church was closed to parishioners and the general public alike; it was locked and unheated. The Catholic grammar school next door had long since been sold to developers and the rectory across the street turned into luxury apartments. But today, there were cars parked on both sides of the street; there were limousines double-parked in front of the church, and police officers in dress uniforms and white gloves directing traffic.

Gary walked up the marble steps, flicked his cigarette into a rhododendron shrub by the front entrance, and opened the heavy wooden door. Inside it was dark, redolent with the odors of old oak, floor polish, candle wax and incense. He dipped two fingers in the holy water font and blessed himself. Lt. McGuire did the same. They parted at the entrance, though; McGuire to take up his station at the back of the church so he could keep his eye on the comings and goings of the mourners, while Gary followed an usher to his reserved pew where the Governor, his grandmother and aunt, dignitaries from the university and politicians were seated. When he sat down, his grandmother accepted his kiss on the cheek, the Governor reached over and shook his hand, and the city manager nodded his condolences. Victoria sat staring straight ahead either lost in prayer or, more likely, thought Gary, in contemplation of her next real estate sale.

The organ began with a requiem and two priests dressed in black and gold entered with the bishop. His peaked miter sat atop his head like the cornet of a medieval prince. He used the gold crosier, his badge of office as pastor of the flock, as a walking stick as he headed toward the altar. Bishop Sullivan was tall and heavy-set. His hands were large and meaty as a longshoreman's but soft and delicate since they had never seen manual labor. His vestments were gold and silver-trimmed and costly, his gray hair stylish, and his freshly-shaved face ruddy and self-assured. His blue eyes sparkled with benevolence and well-fed contentment. He wielded the gold crosier with authority, pointing the priests to their posts. One of the priests carried a thurible which was smoking with burning charcoal and sweet-smelling incense. The bishop nudged him so that the smoke flowed away from his Excellency's eyes. Then the choir struck up a hymn in Latin, "*Veni Creator Spiritus*," and when it was done the Bishop began to chant the opening psalm which began the Mass. *Et introibo ad altare Dei* and the two priests responded *Ad Deum de laetificat joventutem meum.* "And I will go to the altar of God/To God who giveth joy to my youth."

Gary enjoyed hearing the Mass in Latin and he knew that his grandmother must have arranged it. Ever since Vatican II and reversion to the vernacular, parishioners such as his own father had left the Church in droves. Beautiful Latin hymns were replaced by tuneless (and unsingable) hymns in English with banal lyrics. His own father had loved the old Mass and had been an altar boy. His love of Latin and recitations from Virgil and Horace was part of what gave Gary his love of languages.

Gary had taken advantage of this interlude to think of his father. He had so few memories of being really close to him. The old man was often travelling and he and Gary seldom spent what was today called "quality time" together. But now, as the priest intoned the words of the *Pater Noster*, there was one memory which blindsided him with all the poignancy and power of irretrievable loss.

He and his father were playing catch in the back yard one Sunday evening. His father was still in his jacket and tie, just back from a recent trip. With the tie loosened, the jacket flapping in the breeze, his father looked like a young Frank Sinatra, dark and handsome. Gary was practicing his pitching and his father was taking the son's best pitches and winging the hard ball back. Gary must have been nine or ten then. He remembered he was not yet an adolescent because he felt joy that the game was still going on, long after his mother had called him inside to take his bath, a demand that ceased when he was twelve and he took showers—not baths-- when he felt like it.

Dusk had arrived and the streetlights had gone on. Still they played and, as the darkness became more and more palpable, the throws got shorter and shorter as they came closer to each other, each shortening his throws until they were only a few feet away. Then Gary threw down his glove and hugged his father, and his father hugged him back. As they walked back to the house in the darkness with only a crescent moon to light their way, he looked up into his father's eyes and saw the shine of love. It was the closest he would ever feel to the old man. After that came adolescence, his mother's death from cancer, and his father gone to work in Latin America leaving Gary behind at boarding school. His contact with his father in the twenty years since had been brief and usually adversarial. So many of those years wasted....

Now he was slowly finding his way back, looking for something to give his life meaning and purpose. He wiped the tears from his eyes and realized that he could no longer blame his father for who he was. He listened to the chorus as it boomed out the ending lines of the Lord's Prayer like a mantra: *Et ne nos inducas in tentationem, sed libera nos a malo.* Deliver us from evil. He glanced over at his grandmother and she looked back at him. When she saw him wipe his eyes and she reached over and squeezed his hand. He smiled sadly. Soon he would have to ask her about Pilar and the cousin. Soon he would have to perhaps hurt those who remained, however tenuously, his family. But not yet.

When the Last Gospel was completed, the bishop descended the altar and the two priests followed. The altar boy handed the aspergillum to the priest who followed the Bishop around the casket. The bishop dipped it in the water from time to time to bless the front rows of the congregation and then walked around the casket which he also blessed. Then he took the thurible from the other priest, raised it and drew it back and forth against its gold chain three times. Each time a cloud of spicy smoke arose from the censer. The choir began the *"Dies Irae"* and the priest recited the lyrics in Latin as he stood by the coffin. "I am in fear and trembling at the judgment to come, that day of wrath, when heaven and earth shall be moved and the Lord will come to judge the world by fire."

He handed the thurifer by its chains to the assisting priest and walked over to shake hands with Gary, his grandmother and Victoria. He nodded to the Governor and the city manager and then walked majestically, like a medieval prince, back to the sacristy where he bowed briefly in front of the tabernacle, then turned and blessed the congregation. He held out his hands as Gary had seen Christ do in the famous painting where he multiplied the fishes and the loaves. *Dominus vobiscum,* he intoned. Then, *Ite missa est.* And then the chorus and the congregation sang out their gratitude, which echoed against the faux-stone pillars throughout the old church: *Deo gracias.*

The bishop looked over at Gary, his grandmother and Victoria and said, "May the soul of Michael Regan and the souls of all the faithfully departed through the mercy of God rest in peace." And the congregation responded, "Amen." Then, so quickly he almost left his entourage in disarray, the bishop exited to the vestry. There was no sermon. No memorial words. Kennedy was not there. Chomsky, he heard, was in Europe. The pallbearer wheeled the casket down the aisle and out to a waiting hearse. Gary looked at his watch. The whole service took less than thirty-five minutes.

After shaking hands and exchanging hugs with at least three dozen people whom he'd never met, including the Austrian professor from Boston University and the Bolivian general, he finally managed to reach McGuire at the back of the church. McGuire extended his condolences again and then reminded him of what he had said at breakfast.

"We've still got no clue as to where that Guatemalan kid took off to. So, see if you can get some information from the maid. What's her name? Pilar? She's liable to be at your grandmother's now, setting up the buffet for the folks when they get back from the cemetery."

"Yeah, okay," Gary said, a bit worried as he looked over to the hearse and the limousines lining up in front of the church. "But I should be going out to the burial as well."

"Look," McGuire urged, a bit impatient now but also understanding. "Head over to your grandmother's right now. It's only up the block. I'll have the traffic detail take their time getting the motorcycle escort lined up. Your grandmother is talking to the Bishop and she'll be here for a while longer."

Gary came through the back door of his grandmother's house behind one of the waiters from the catering service. Pilar was in the living room directing the placement of the buffet and the chaffing dishes.

"*Buenos días*, Pilar."

"Hola, Señor Gary. You startled me! You are not out at the *campo santo? Que pasó?*"

"No, I am headed there almost immediately but something came up that was extremely urgent. I need to ask you about your cousin."

"Juan Manuel?" She looked frightened. "What about him? Is he in trouble?

"Why would you think that, Pilar?" Gary asked suspiciously.

"Because he has not been home in two days. I have been very worried."

"Do you have any idea where he might have gone?"

"No. But all of last week he was preoccupied. And once I saw him talking to a fat ugly man who looked like a *jefe*, although he was dressed in workman's clothes. I asked Juan Manuel who he was and he said a foreman on his job. I asked him if he was in trouble on his job and he said no. But something was troubling him."

"So the last time you saw him was two nights ago."

"Yes. He said that he had a ticket to the Folk Festival at Fort Adam's State Park. He said he got a ticket from the Madam."

"Which Madam would that be, Pilar?"

"Why, I thought you knew, Señor Gary. My cousin works for your Aunt Victoria at Regan and Stein, the real estate company. He helps clean up her properties before showings."

CHAPTER EIGHTEEN

On her twelve-hour flight down to Bolivia, Teresa read the *Lonely Planet* guide to the country. She was surprised to find that the territory was so vast. She knew, of course, that Brazil was the size of the continental United States, which made her journey south longer than that of a flight to Europe. But she thought of Bolivia as a tiny country. In fact, despite the loss of half of its territory and an outlet to the sea from losing wars with Chile, Paraguay and Brazil, Bolivia was still the fifth largest country in South America. It was three and a half times the size of Great Britain. Sparsely populated, its seven and a half million people accounted for a density of only twenty persons per square mile.

She read that almost sixty percent of the population was indigenous. And that, despite its enormous wealth in gold, silver, tin, coca, sugar cane and natural gas, it was also the poorest per capita, one of the most volatile politically, and had the fewest number of tourists.

When she arrived at the El Alto airport to change planes for the final leg to Santa Cruz, there were airport personnel standing by with oxygen tanks. At 13,000 feet La Paz was one of the highest airports in the world. The dangers of deplaning range from dizziness and nausea to pulmonary or even cerebral embolism. Teresa, however, felt fine, and had only an hour to wait until the TAM jet loaded up for the short flight to the southern city.

It was early morning when she arrived in Santa Cruz. The airport was crowded and noisy with dozens of hotel and corporate representatives holding up cardboard signs for the passengers coming through customs. Dr. Carlos Rivera from the Faculdad del Derecho of the Universidad Privada de Santa Cruz had said that he would meet her plane, so she looked around hoping to see her name on a sign. Then she heard her name called, and the young, energetic professor with a hand-lettered sign came bustling over to where she stood. He gave her a welcoming embrace, a kiss on both cheeks, and picked up her luggage.

"My car is just outside," he said, speaking rapidly in Spanish. "I am Carlos Rivera Quintero. How wonderful to see you! We are all so sorry for your loss. Michael Regan was so important here in Bolivia. He was doing very valuable work. We all feel this is a great loss. But I am talking too much. How was your trip? It was quite long, no? Nothing is easy in Latin America."

"Thank you so much for meeting me, Carlos," replied Teresa, also in Spanish. "The trip was not so difficult, although I could use a cup of coffee."

"Yes, say no more. I will treat you to the best coffee in Bolivia. Very strong, so thick you will have to add hot water and milk to cut it. But first let me take you to your hotel. There you can wash up and relax yourself. It is not too far. We will have coffee in the restaurant there and talk a bit. Then, if you are up for it, we will go out to dinner tonight and you can meet some of Michael's colleagues and friends."

He loaded her luggage into a dusty Land Rover and drove out of the airport parking lot.

"I will be your tourist guide, no?" he said as they swung out onto the highway. "And if you don't mind, I would like to practice my English."

"I would love you to be my guide," Teresa smiled. "There is so much to know about this beautiful country and I will not be here very long. And English is fine. It is actually my first language. I was not born in Mexico even though my husband and I have lived there many years."

"Ah, but you speak so well...although it is true with a bit of an accent—still much better than mine in English. Well, let me begin. Santa Cruz is the richest city in Bolivia. Many wealthy families, land owners and businessmen are living here. The city is about one and a half *millones*. It is roughly oval in shape and divided into four *anillos* or *como se dice*...rings with *radiales*...um

"Spokes?" she offered.

"Yes, exactly, with spokes that connect the rings. We are leaving the Viru-Viru Airport and it is in the outer ring and this highway is the *Radial Numero Uno*. We will arrive to the *Primer Anillo,* which is downtown, in about thirty minutes. A quick ride, really, although it may be bumpy. Santa Cruz is a very rich city, we are very proud of that. But still, less that 30% of our streets and highways are paved so we have mucho *polvo*, you know...um, dust, and in *las lluvias*, the season of rains, much flooding and mud."

They arrived at the Hotel Las Americas in less than half an hour. She checked in, unpacked her bag, and washed up while Carlos waited for her in the hotel restaurant. When she was refreshed she joined him there. He rose to greet her, again giving her the traditional double kiss on both cheeks. She noted that he had to spring up a bit on his toes to be comfortable. Thin, and less than five foot five, Carlos was two inches shorter than she. Teresa was not particular fond of short Latin men who tended to be macho and pushy, but Carlos was the exception. He had lively black eyes, a warm smile, and an irrepressible energy that Teresa found attractive. He gestured quietly to the waiter who rolled a silver coffee tray over to their table.

The coffee was everything Teresa had been led to expect. It was almost syrupy in its thickness, and the waiter served both hot water and hot milk to dilute it. After the first couple of sips she felt an incredible caffeine rush which dissolved the exhaustion of the flight in a rich odor of Arabica. Carlos passed her a basket of sweet rolls. "For your digestion," he said. "Our coffee is quite strong on an empty stomach."

"So why did Michael come to work down here?" Teresa asked. "I mean he was a pretty dynamic professor and had some pull in academia, especially in Latin America. So why didn't he go to the Catholic University of Chile or Los Altos in Colombia? I mean, no disrespect, but Bolivia is not known for having any notable universities."

Carlos frowned. "Well, it depends on what you mean by notable, of course. We have no MIT or Harvard or London School of Economics, but we do have access to the best research and we have outstanding professors. In Bolivia, the best universities are in Santa Cruz, which is why Michael chose this city rather than La Paz or Cochabamba. And, yes, the pay is poor and the facilities are less than he was accustomed to either in the U.S. or even Mexico or Chile. We are not Georgetown or Tec de Monterrey or Universidad Católica de Chile, nothing like those. No great laboratories or libraries. But we have good researchers, good exchange agreements with foreign universities, especially Germany and Canada. We also have an excellent wireless system for dependable Internet access."

"But still…there must have been something else to attract someone of his reputation who could pretty much choose where he wished to work," Teresa protested.

"Well, yes and no. First, of all you know that Michael was a socialist. Opportunities for such professors are almost non-existent in the U.S. For example, Chomsky at MIT, who appears to be an exception, is actually a professor of semantics whose work goes back to the Fifties and who has been tenured in that department for forty years. If he were to apply to MIT today as say, a professor of economics, he wouldn't stand a chance of getting hired. So Michael had to choose a progressive university.

"The other factor is that Santa Cruz is a crucible of social, economic and political change. Things are happening here which will affect the whole world. In North America they have a much distorted view of the effects of globalization. Some lost jobs, perhaps. Some poor quality toys from China, the shrinking of the middle class, global warming. They have Lou Dobbs who gives the public heavy doses of xenophobia and colorful anti-immigration diatribes which distract people from the real issue."

"And what exactly *is* the real issue?" Teresa asked.

"The real issue is the gradual erosion of democracy around the world, not by dictators or Marxists, not even by populists like Chávez. It is being accomplished by multinational corporations which are devastating the forests, creating irreversible climate change, privatizing natural resources such as water, eliminating indigenous people, and controlling elections by withdrawing their support from any politician who does not support their corporate agenda. You can't see that very clearly if you look at a global model. Or even at the U.S. model which is purposely complex and media-controlled so that the public probably wouldn't see it anyway. But Santa Cruz is a micro-model in which all the factors are very clear, very easy to observe and study."

"Did you get your education here, Carlos?"

"Just high school. I was a student at the Cooperative School of Santa Cruz, an American-style bilingual school. My father was a consul from Paraguay. When I graduated I received a scholarship to Notre Dame and I studied economics there. They I returned to Latin America and earned a dual doctorate of laws from the Universidad Católica de Chile and the University of Heidelberg. It was there that I met your father-in-law."

"In Germany?"

"No, in Santiago, Chile. Heidelberg has a law center there. You study the Chilean law program during the school year and then spend summers in Germany. I attended one of Professor Regan's-- Michael's-- lectures in Santiago. Brilliant! I knew that I would find a way to work with him if I could.

"So when the rector told me that he was offering Michael a position here, I knew the salary would be less than attractive. I knew I had to step up to help sweeten the pot. I managed to persuade Emma Lee, who is here on exchange from the University of British Columbia working on her doctorate, to be his assistant. And I offered to be his attorney, and handle the ramifications of his proposals."

"So, you're his lawyer as well?"

"That's correct," he smiled, opening his briefcase and pulling out a thick file folder. "And I know you brought a power of attorney. So, if you'd like we can get to his will right now and that will leave us free to discuss other less personal matters at dinner. May I see your power of attorney?"

Teresa reached into her purse and pulled out a business-sized envelope which contained the legal document. Carlos scanned it briefly and put it in his file. He then passed her a sealed manila envelope.

She opened it and scanned the top two sheets. They were written in Spanish, in accessible though legalistic language.

"He leaves most of his estate to your husband, Gary, as you can see. A small house, not worth much, maybe $80,000; a 2001 Dodge Neon and a bank account with about $10,000. But he also leaves stock in CITCO, the Venezuelan oil company.

"I see, Teresa said reading over the documents.

"Do you? The stocks are worth approximately 1.6 million in U.S. currency at current rates of exchange. Your father-in-law left you and your husband very well off."

"My God! More than one and a half million?"

"Yes, and increasing in value every day. They could be worth double that if oil goes to over $140 a barrel, which it's predicted to do by the end of the year."

Teresa grew thoughtful. "Well that's wonderful news. But something puzzles me. Making this will," she held up the four pages which comprised the document, "would not have been much work, Carlos. What other kind of legal work did you do for Michael? You mentioned something about 'the ramifications of his proposals.' What exactly did that entail?"

Carlos finished his coffee, and then dabbed his lips with the linen napkin. "Ah, but that is too long a story for me to go into now, Teresa. Why don't I come back about seven o'clock and take you out to dinner? Michael's assistant, Emma, will join us and she can tell you a bit more about Michael's work. I'm sure you'll find it all very interesting."

CHAPTER NINETEEN

K en Beebe felt he had a pretty cushy job, even though it only paid nine bucks an hour. He was a Park Ranger III, the supervisor on graveyard shift at Fort Adams State Park. The historic site, situated near the eastern entrance to Narragansett Bay, three miles southwest of Newport, was remote and quiet after dark, and his responsibilities as supervising ranger were not at all taxing. Mostly, Beebe told the other rangers what to do, walked around a bit if it was pleasant weather, filled a shift report, and trained a seasonal park ranger, a college kid assigned to him for the summer.

Fort Adams was a 105-acre fortification built in the mid-1800s and one of the largest such installations in the United States. It was designed for the mounting of 468 cannons and supported a wartime garrison of 2,400 men. Its complex architecture, casements, tunnels and bastions occupied the hands of hundred of Irish stone masons working in brick and granite for almost thirty years. It was important strategically because Narragansett Bay was considered the best harbor on the east coast, and the only one accessible in a northeast gale by either American ships or an enemy's. After serving the army for over a century and the Navy for almost two decades, the fort was finally ceded to the State and converted into a historic park and recreation area. Its six-acre parade field was now the site of the Newport Jazz and Folk Festivals.

Tonight there was a chill in the air so Ranger Beebe had gone over to the Eisenhower House to stay warm. He was looking through the library of the President's summer home, checking out the World War II memorabilia, when his radio crackled. It was the college kid, calling in a suspicious odor coming from one of many underground tunnels which connected the abandoned ammunition storerooms and army barracks.

"Is it one that is locked or one that's open to the public?

"A locked one, sir. The chain and padlock are still there. The padlock appears to have been tampered with. I also think I hear the sounds of rats squeaking in there."

"Shit. Okay, make a note of that for day shift. We need to get some exterminators over there tomorrow. We can't have rats scaring the tourists. Listen, did you shine your light in there? Can you see anything that the rats might be after?"

One of his fears was that with the elimination of low cost housing in Newport, he might run into some homeless person who decided to camp out in one of the seldom used tunnels, some bum who'd leave his trash and food behind to attract rodents.

"Well, sir, I can't see all the way in. But it does appear that there's a bundle of rags just at the bend in the tunnel."

The bundle of rags turned out to be a Hispanic boy in his late teens. When the police arrived and lit up the scene, it was apparent to the CSI, Linda Hempel, that the victim had been there had been there long enough for decomposition to have set in. Of course, it would have been hot in there during the day. And the rats had indeed been at him. There was no sign of trauma, however.

Pete McGuire caught the homicide code and was there within twenty minutes just as the CSI was finishing up.

Hempel, a competent but often irascible woman in her thirties who had been passed over for promotion twice, looked up when he came in. She brushed back her blond hair with stubby fingers and looked at him with tired eyes. It was four a.m. and she had been out partying until two. It felt like she had just crawled into bed when the call came in.

"What have you got, Linda?" he asked, looking down at the victim then stepping back quickly as the decomposition odor rose up and made his gorge rise.

"Hispanic male, seventeen, maybe eighteen years old."

"What else did you find?"

"Well, she said, there is no evidence of any trauma; no stab wounds, bullet holes or blunt force evidence. But…." she raised the boy's left arm, "I did find a couple of needle marks on the victim's arm. You can also see that there's a slight swelling, a bump as if he had tried to hit the vein and had missed and then tried again. The medical examiner will confirm, of course, but it looks to me like an overdose."

"Possible, I guess," Pete said, looking around at the tunnel and then at the gate. He took another look at the boy's arm. "But no tracks, only these two punctures. Odd he would overdose. Not a sign that he was a habitual user."

"It only takes one time, if you get hold of some bad dope," Linda remarked.

"Yeah, or if someone gets hold of it for you," McGuire quipped over his shoulder.

He walked over to interview Ranger Beebe and the college kid who found the body. He felt certain that he knew who the victim

A DEATH IN NEWPORT

was. He fit the description of his Guatemalan suspect and McGuire was certain that the fingerprints would confirm it.

"Was the gate locked or unlocked when you checked it?" Pete asked the summer trainee, a skinny kid with glasses and a uniform shirt whose collar was too large.

"It was locked, Sir. I tried it but the chain was around it and the padlock was closed."

"You're sure."

"Yessir," added Beebe stepping up. "I arrived at the scene immediately after I got the call. Didn't touch anything but I did unlock the gate, went over to check the body. A first I thought it was just a bundle of clothes left by some bum sleeping in there. Then I saw it was some Mexican kid and the rats had been at him. Shit. Don't know what he could have been doing in there."

"Guatemalan," McGuire said briskly.

"What?"

"I said, the victim was a Guatemalan, not a Mexican," he snapped with ill-concealed annoyance.

"Yeah, whatever. They're all Latinos, right? But he sure as hell had locked himself in there," Lieutenant. Guess he figured he'd fool Security. Probably would have worked, too, if my summer intern here hadn't noticed a smell."

McGuire turned them both over to the uniforms to give a statement. Then he walked off and thought about it. He needed a cup of coffee.

It might make sense for the kid to go in there to fix, if he was trying to find a spot where he'd be undetected. But would the kid pick the lock, undo the chain, and then lock himself in again? Possible, if he wanted to deceive security. Still....he thought it somehow unlikely. He might just close the hasp so it would look locked, but leave it open so he could make a quick exit.

Gary and Tommy awoke early and had a breakfast of Raisin Bran, toast and coffee. Then they refilled their cups, took their cigarettes and went out on the fire escape. Gary read the morning meditation and prayer from the Twenty-Four Hour book to set the tone for the day.

"It's going be a good day, Tommy. We'll go for a walk on the cliffs; you can show me where you found the fishing pole. Then we'll drop off your affidavit, have lunch, and go to a meeting."

"By the time we get back, maybe your wife will call," Tommy said.

"Yeah, I'm not too worried. She was going out to dinner last night with some of my dad's colleagues. She said she had some good news to report."

They finished their smokes and then headed down to the Cliff Walk at the end of Ruggles. They walked quickly past the protected estates, down the paved areas, and then more slowly as they descended the less developed path leading to the tunnels. Along the way, Tommy pointed out the wildflowers and shrubs along the way.

"This one is pretty," Gary, said, pointing to a two foot tall plant with pale flowers. "What is it?"

"Well, most people call it loosestrife; others call it purple loosestrife although the flowers are sort of a lavender. The yellow one next to it with the pods is wild flax. Here, see if you can guess what this one is. He picked some leaves from a plant with a purple flower with slender spikes, and handed them to Gary.

"No? Then try crushing the leaves in your hand, and then smell them."

"Ahh. It's mint!"

"Yes, *menta piperita*. Mint or peppermint. This is a rich area for flora. And over here we can tell there was a grass fire, probably last season. These large purple flowers are evening primrose and they invade after a burn."

They went through two tunnels and as they came up the other side Tommy stopped by several large clumps of poison ivy which even Gary recognized, with their shiny three-leaf clusters.

"I know what this is. 'Leaves of three, let it be,'" he added quoting from memory the Boy Scout Handbook. "But I don't ever remember the leaves being this big or the plants so high."

"One of the lesser-known effects of global warming. You see," Tommy explained, "as the earth gets warmer, CO_2 levels rise dramatically. Some plants thrive on CO_2, and poison ivy is one of them. The size of the plants, the number of plants and even the urioshol resin has risen thirty-three percent in the past decade."

"Urioshol?" Gary asked.

"That's the oil that causes the poison ivy rash. It's much more powerful now than it was when we were kids, and results in much more vigorous rashes. Some are so bad that they end up disfiguring the victim. Young kids are especially vulnerable. Anyway…here's where I found the fishing rod. In that big clump of poison ivy just at the corner."

Gary took out a pad and made a small diagram.

"And where is Rough Point from here?

"Just a few hundred yards," Tommy said.

Gary wrote some notes on his pad.

"And your father's body was found on that little beach below there where those plovers are."

Gary looked down and saw some tiny shorebirds running across the sand. He would have guessed them to be sandpipers, but the more he listened to Tommy the more he was convinced of his encyclopedic knowledge. So, plovers they were. He also figured

Tommy would tell him about his past in his own good time. He already knew that he had been a teacher and, by his enthusiasm and knowledge, it was obvious to Gary that he was a pretty good one. *What could have happened? Well,* he chided himself, *the alcohol happened, obviously.*

He asked Tommy to give him a few minutes alone and then scrambled down the slope to the small beach, scattering the young birds. He squatted down on the sand and said a small prayer for his father. The tide had washed away any traces of what had happened here just a few nights ago. *Time and tide,* his grandmother used to say, *wait for no man.*

The walk back would have been uneventful were it not for Tommy keeping up his enthusiastic description of the flora as they passed.

"Watch it! More poison ivy," Gary said, skirting another tangle of three-leafed vines along the path.

"Nope," Tommy stopped picking up the vine. "The three-leaf configuration is what caught your attention. But notice the presence of thorns along the stems. This vine is raspberry, probably a cutting from one of the estate gardens that took root when the gardener dumped his prunings over the wall. And, ah, this is something you might want to add to your medicine kit if you intended to hike this area very often."

"What is it?" Gary asked, looking at the yellow flowers with red dots. Tommy popped the seeds in some of the flowers as he handed them to him.

"Jewelweed," Tommy smiled. "It's the only known cure for poison ivy. And the irony of it is that it is also a preventive. If you do happen to get it, putting the jewelweed on your skin after the exposure will significantly reduce both the area of rash and the duration. But if you know ahead of time that you're going to an area where there's poison ivy, rubbing the liquid from the stems on your skin will prevent you from ever getting it."

"But how come it's not bottled and sold?"

"Because the pharmaceutical companies make money off people's misery, not off their good health. Come on," Tommy argued impatiently. "The whole point of the medical community in this country is to profit from people's afflictions, not to prevent them. I think that should be obvious by now. Haven't you seen the Michael Moore documentary, *Sicko*? The most expensive mansion in America is owned by the CEO of a pharmaceutical corporation. He didn't get there by bottling jewelweed, and probably would hire helicopters to spray DDT or Agent Orange to eliminate it if he found it growing anywhere near his estate."

"When did we get to the point where these people control our country?" Gary asked.

"When we lost faith in common sense, and the belief that an ordinary person with ordinary intelligence and courage could make a difference. Even a reformed drunk with two days of sobriety knows that."

"*Especially* a reformed drunk, I'd say." Gary added. "Too bad more straight people can't see that. It could change the world."

CHAPTER TWENTY

D riving out in the Land Rover, Carlos and Teresa passed the tennis courts of the hotel. They had been flooded during the previous night's storm and now, though the waters had receded, they were covered in a thick red mud. *Gary wouldn't like that*, Teresa thought, remembering how her husband played tennis in every country they visited in Latin America and judged each country accordingly. But when they arrived at the restaurant, she had a pleasant surprise. Given the dirt streets and the generally rundown appearance of the neighborhood, Miguel Angelo's seemed even more elegant than Carlos had suggested. It was like a flawless gem in a rough setting. Decorated in Spanish colonial style with oil paintings, heavy carved ornate furniture and comfortable cushions, it was dark and candlelit. The staff was polite and helpful without being overbearing or obsequious.

The hostess escorted them to their table where a Chinese woman in her late twenties awaited them. Dressed in a simple black shift, she was tall and willowy but with muscle tone suggesting she worked out regularly. Her black hair was cropped short, and a pair of horn-rimmed eyeglasses barely disguised her obvious beauty and perfect cheekbones.

"Teresa, may I present Emma Lee? Emma, this is Michael's daughter-in-law," Carlos said formally after kissing the young Asian woman on both cheeks.

They exchanged pleasantries and then ordered drinks. When the waiter went to the bar, Carlos explained to Teresa the importance of Emma's work.

"When Michael came to Bolivia he knew a bit about the historical background but most of his contemporary understanding was generalized," Carlos explained. "He thought that Evo Morales, as an avowed socialist, would put into practice many of the ideas which Chávez had adopted in Venezuela: expropriation of large estates, giving small arable parcels of land to peasants, providing price supports to basic commodities, reducing the power of the landed gentry, and distribution of wealth."

"It's what many people thought at the time," Emma interjected. "Although now we have reason to believe that Chávez knew the truth. Morales, though ostensibly a member of the socialist party and an indigenous person himself, had no intention of making those kinds of reforms. In fact, he was very much in league with the large corporations, especially agribusiness, which helped put him in power."

"What Emma discovered in her research," Carlos said picking up the narrative, "is that the rates of forest exploitation in Bolivia have exceeded even those of Brazil. More than 11% of the forests here have been destroyed by logging and agribusiness as compared with 8% in Brazil. Most of the land is being sold off by the Bolivian government at about 25 cents per acre ostensibly to give the landless indigenous people farms. And, of course, this is what you hear in the news stories. But what you see when you travel the country is something entirely different."

"The land is being bought up in enormous parcels by cooperatives organized by the Japanese, the Chinese and the Mennonites," Emma added. "They then clear-cut vast tracts of land and plant soybeans and other export crops in meticulously-tended fields that extend for miles. They have these huge farms that look like something you'd see in Iowa or Ohio. But what happens after a couple of years is that heavy winds and rains deplete the acidic forest soils, and these owners abandon the farms, get a tax credit from the government for their losses, buy new land at rock bottom prices and begin again. They leave the depleted land ravaged, and the indigenous people starving. None of the land goes to grow food for the people of Bolivia. It is all used to grow export crops with the profits going to multinationals and their Japanese intermediaries."

"All of these people have contracts with large agribusiness concerns," Carlos explained. "These conglomerates are the real power, not the government or the Asian developers. And what is happening here is far more destructive that other historical examples of exploitation, whether the Belgians in the Congo, or the Spanish in the Americas. Emma was convinced that Chávez knew all this, and that our Michael Regan was sent here to put a monkey wrench in the works."

"But now, I'm not so sure," Emma said. When Carlos told me the details of Michael's will and the 1.6 million in CITCO stocks it appeared that it might be the case and the stocks a reward for his service. However, with his death, it seems more likely that Chávez felt that Michael was becoming a liability in Caracas, too much of an idealist and a gringo one at that. Certainly not the type of advisor he'd want in the forefront of a populist revolution. My feeling now is that he used him the same way Castro used Che Guevara."

"What do you mean?" asked Teresa, a bit overwhelmed by these Byzantine revelations.

"Well, Guevara if you remember was an Argentine, hence his nickname 'Che' which means 'buddy' in the Argentine idiom. When he talked about extending the socialist revolution throughout the region, Fidel decided he was too dangerous. Castro was a nationalist, not an ideologue. So he encouraged Che to go off to Bolivia with a handful of men to start a peasant revolution there. The so-called Bolivian revolution never got off the ground. Che was hunted down by the Bolivian army and killed, not too far from here."

"Tomorrow, if you like, we'll go see where Che died," Carlos interjected. "There is a large memorial there now. I will also show you our largest national forest which was once a birthright of the people, much like your Yellowstone National Park. It is now a third destroyed by tractors and earthmovers since the government opened it up to agribusiness under the euphemism 'multiple land use.' But that's enough talk," Carlos concluded abruptly. "You must be starving after your trip and here we have the best food in the city."

Teresa ordered the chicken breast, breaded and layered with sage, prosciutto, mozzarella, and then smothered in a creamy mushroom sauce; along with a half bottle of dry white Bolivian wine. She felt a guilty pleasure at ordering the wine, since she had always refrained from drinking at dinner ever since Gary got sober. But he was not here now and there was the feeling she'd had when she first went off to college and had her first drink in a bar, that of being slightly naughty.

They talked mostly about their food, Emma's veal saltimbocca and Carlos' wild mushroom risotto. The quiet, meditative atmosphere of the restaurant was like a medieval retreat. She was surprised that neither ordered the seafood and Emma explained that Bolivia was a landlocked country and, while you could get seafood flown in frozen, it was not the same as fresh. She talked about the seafood restaurants in Vancouver where she grew up, and how her parents had immigrated to Canada after Hong Kong was turned over to the Chinese.

Carlos ordered double espressos for them all and then they chose desserts which they could share from the pastry cart. When the coffee arrived along with spumoni, raspberry cheesecake, and cannoli, Teresa risked asking a question that had been troubling her.

"So, do the indigenous people at least get jobs when these parcels of land are bought up and turned into mega-farms?"

Carlos looked at Emma. She nodded for him to go ahead and answer. "Well, yes, in a perverted sense. Although much of the work is with big machines, especially the clearing and so on, there are many unskilled laborers who work the fields. We suspect that many of them are held in a kind of peonage. They are brought in from other parts of the country and housed on the estates."

"And recently we have seen young men employed as guards on some of the large estates whom I believe are brought in from Central America." Emma added.

"How do you know they are from Central America?

"I was in a small *puesto* near the national forest a couple of months ago. There was a very rude young man who approached me, flirting. The Spanish he was using was not Bolivian. It had many vulgar terms we do not use. My guess was that it was kind of prison slang. Then I saw a tattoo on his arm. It said M-13. When I got back to my office I researched it on the Internet. It is the tattoo of a very deadly Central American gang called the Mara Salvatruchas. They are very powerful in El Salvador, Honduras, and especially in Guatemala where they now number in the tens of thousands."

"Guatemala? That's a long way from Bolivia. What on earth would they be doing in Santa Cruz?"

"Our question exactly, and we are not sure. We only know that they are here and someone hired them. Michael and I were investigating that and we were close to an answer." Emma said. "I do know he had been warned by several people that he should back off. Gently, by some well-meaning people connected to the university, and by others not so gentle or well-meaning connected to the developers. It was why I was so relieved when Michael decided to go up north to attend the conference. I felt at least he would be safe. There are no Guatemalans in Rhode Island."

CHAPTER TWENTY-ONE

The elegantly-dressed Latino at the burial service held himself stiffly, his back ramrod straight, his face impassive, as he watched the body slowly lowered into the grave. Only the sadness in his eyes revealed the depth of his grief. He waited until most of the mourners had left before he walked over and placed a single white rose on the casket as it was lowered into the ground.

He walked over to Gary and bowed slightly. "I wish to extend again my deepest sympathies. Professor Regan was a good man, a friend to Bolivia, and his loss is inestimable."

"Thank you, General," Gary replied. He had met Brigadier Hector Domínguez earlier at the church but they had no time to talk then. Gary had been rushing over to his grandmother's house to question Pilar and their meeting was perfunctory though Gary was very curious about the general's business in Newport and the connection, if any, with his father. Now, he got right to the point.

"Dr. Alioto from the Pell Center told me that you are attending a conference at the Naval War College and that you might have some information for me."

"Perhaps we could go for a walk," the general replied, and gestured respectfully toward where the workers had begun filling in the grave. Gary nodded his head in agreement and together they hiked up a small grassy knoll which looked out over Narragansett Bay.

"Such a beautiful day and such a lovely spot," the general remarked in a soft voice. He turned to Gary with a rueful smile. The sadness Gary observed, looking into his eyes, was genuine.

"It makes the loss of Professor Regan even more poignant. As I said, your father was a good man. He was very concerned with the exploitation, some would call it peonage, of the Bolivian workers. He discovered several anomalies that the army was investigating. One was that a number of Guatemalan gang members were being used as labor camp guards and enforcers. The other was a series of events which pointed to a conspiracy between several corporations and politicians to take over national forest lands for bio-fuel agriculture. Your father had evidence that there was a land-owner's cartel which was behind these activities. He had identified a couple of individuals who were in the lower echelon. We had hoped he would be able to expose the higher levels which we had reason to believe reached all the way to the top of the government, including congressional leaders and maybe even the president himself.

"But then a number of mistakes were made. My superiors felt that this was a job for the national police. The army is not, after all, an investigative branch or a law enforcement agency. In the process of turning the case over to them I think some information was leaked by their agents, or by politicians who had been questioned by them. At any rate, your father's investigations became known to people who could very well have been in a position to silence him.

"I was concerned. But then your father was invited to come to the Pell Center and, coincidentally, I was invited to attend a series of seminars on international security at the War College. So, there we were. Both of us in Newport and far from Santa Cruz. It did not occur to me at the time that perhaps this could have been arranged by people who wanted us both out of the country. Nor, am I certain even now that it was. Only...."

"Did something change which made you feel there was a plan to get you both out of Bolivia?"

"Well, one of the individuals whom your father had identified as a capo or mid-level boss for the land developers was a thug by the name of Cesar Castillo. We had heard reports of Castillo in the past. There were rumors that he was brutalizing native men, raping women. But no formal charges were ever brought. In the region where he operates, he and men like him effectively *are* the law. The few times we had contact with him, once when uncovering a weapons cache, another time when there was violence at a clear-cutting site and some demonstrators had been badly beaten, we were called off by my military superiors. It seems that this Castillo, the worst kind of white man, is well-protected."

"He's a white man?" Gary asked. "An American?"

"No, not a *North* American. But there are many white men in South America, as you should well know," he chided gently. "But this one, a fat slug, with a German mother and an Andalusian father, is a creature who has complete contempt for the indigenous people and their cultures, and even less respect for the land."

"So, how does he come into the picture? He was in Santa Cruz. You and my father were in Newport."

"That's just it. The day after your father died, I saw this *cabrón* on Thames Street. He was in one of the shops and I believe he was purchasing a ticket for one of the music concerts. I was certain that it was him, although he was wearing dark glasses and dressed as a day laborer. The traffic was heavy that day and by the time I had crossed the street he had left the store and headed toward the ferry landing. I was too far behind him and when the ferry passengers disembarked, he managed to lose himself in the crowd. I never saw him again."

That night Gary slept fitfully. Earlier the evening had been humid, the air heavy and still with occasional flashes of heat lightning. He turned on the ceiling fans and a standing fan that Carolina had lent him and put them both on full power, but the air continued to be heavy and close in the apartment. He could hear Tommy tossing on his bed across the way. Then, just as he was about to fall asleep, about four in the morning, lightning lit up the room as thunder boomed out in the ocean. Then the rumbling grew louder with lightning striking closer and closer until the bedroom lit up like noonday and the smell of ozone leaked in through the open window along with the rainwater. He got up to shut the window, amid the thunder crack and drumming and flashes of lightning, and felt a strange anxiety as if the storm were somehow personal. He got his feet wet too, so he went to the bathroom to dry them and use the toilet. Tommy was sitting upright in bed. Gary told him grouchily to go back to sleep.

"Nobody can sleep through this noise," Tommy said.

So they both got up and Gary made coffee and they sat together by the window watching the storm, drinking coffee and smoking cigarettes until dawn. And he thought about Teresa and how he missed her, how he hoped that they would be together soon, with all of this resolved. He was curious as to what she would see in Bolivia and what the country was like. He wondered if anything she might experience there would relate to what he was doing in Newport, where nothing seemed to make sense and so many factors seemed to be in collusion against the truth.

- -

Santa Cruz, Bolivia

Teresa, Carlos and Emma had travelled for several hours in the Land Rover before they came upon the first signs of the national forest, which extended for several million acres in every direction. A heavy cloud of acrid blue-gray smoke fell over the trees and covered the dirt road with a suffocating pall. As they turned the corner, heading deeper into the wilderness, she saw the reason: burning brush, charred stumps of trees, and the roar of wood chippers, chain saws and earth moving equipment. For miles in either direction the forest was being burned systematically, then churned up and the land scraped clean for crops. The smoke had begun to burn their eyes and throat, so they put the windows up in the vehicle. Visibility narrowed to a few feet in front of the highlights which Carlos had belatedly turned on as the roadway gradually began to disappear in an acrid cloud of smoke and debris.

"This is horrible," Teresa said. "They are destroying everything!"

"It is called El Chaqueo, the Big Smoke, which comes from the slashing and burning of the rain forest to provide agricultural land. Ten years ago all of this was virgin forest and wilderness; the only way in was by mule or on horseback. Now logging roads cut through the entire region, and it is easily accessible to heavy equipment and earth movers."

"But isn't this horrible destruction against the law?"

"In fact," Carlos replied, "the burning is against the law but there is no one to enforce it. The tree removal and agricultural activities are legal, though. They are now part of what is termed 'multi-use" of the forest. Originally that term meant grazing by a few local cattle. But now it has come to mean everything from mining to agriculture. We estimate that in the past ten years Bolivia has lost more than 45% of its national forests."

The smoke began to clear ten minutes later, as they continued down the logging road which turned into an improved two-lane highway. They came upon enormous green swaths of land, thousands of acres of neat green rows of plants as far as the eye could see. It looked so pristine, so Midwestern American that Teresa almost felt that she had been transported back home.

"This is what happens after the land has been cleared," Carlos told her. "These farms raise mostly soybeans for export; this entire crop will be exported for biofuel or ethanol. An acre of soybeans yields about 60 gallons of fuel. If this keeps up, the United Nations estimates that 98% of Bolivian forest will be gone in the next decade. Meanwhile, the indigenous peoples have either been driven off or put into chattel servitude on their own ancestral lands. Fewer and fewer farms are growing food to be consumed by the people who live here. More and more food is being imported at prices the poor cannot afford.

"In Mexico the same thing is happening with the corn crop," Teresa said. "Over thirty million hectares planted in corn and most of it exported for cattle feed or gone into biofuels. Not surprisingly the price of corn has doubled over the last two years. This winter over a million people in Mexico City protested the doubling of the price of tortillas which is the staple food for the Mexican people. The police and the army put down the protests with tear gas and water cannons imported from the United States. It's really criminal. Crops are going to fill gas tanks instead of people's bellies."

"Yes, Chávez mentioned this problem when Bush was visiting Brazil. Bush was saying how he looked forward to an alliance between North and South America to produce alternative fuels and insure independence from foreign oil. Chávez said, "The Yankees would have us all starve so they can keep their cars running!""

"A bit of an exaggeration, wouldn't you say?" laughed Teresa. "Chávez *is* a bit of a blowhard."

"Characterize him as you will," Carlos said. "The fact remains that most of what he says is true. The U.N. agrees with him and even the head of Tyson Foods in the U.S. has said that reallocation of farmland for biofuel initiatives would cause devastating food shortages around the world."

"Still," Teresa persisted. "These people do have lovely farms. The tiled roofs, the stock ponds, the cattle grazing, and acres and acres of green. It's almost perfect."

"Yes, for about seven years. Then the weak forest soil is depleted of nutrients from the leaching caused by irrigation, then by flooding. Seven years, max. Which is why they are slashing and burning the forest you saw just south of here. Let's drive a bit further and look at the land that was cultivated eight years ago."

When they made the final turn ten miles up the road they came to an area as desolate as the moon. Acres and acres of dust as far as the eye could see. Not a tree or a blade of grass; only some scrub cactus and the occasional cement foundation of a stripped and abandoned farmhouse.

"Oh, my God! There must be thousand of acres of just…a dustbowl, like Oklahoma in the Thirties."

"Not thousand of acres, Teresa. *Millions* of acres. This is the end result of what is called *capitalismo salvaje*, or wild capitalism. And everyone is involved: the politicians, the biofuel promoters, the land developers, the Japanese, the Germans, the Americans, the Bolivian government. They are destroying the land and the people out of pure, unmitigated greed."

"It is so sad," Teresa said.

"Yes," Carlos agreed. "But sadness does not motivate anyone to change it. We need to get angry to do that; we need to be spurred into action. Let's continue on and we will make a pilgrimage to a man who hoped to do just that. He failed, of course, but that should not dissuade us. Like Professor Regan, like Robert Kennedy, he had a dream of how things could be better for the people and he died for it.

They arrived in the little pueblo of Villagrande in the late afternoon. Teresa had seen hand-lettered signs and graffiti announcing "Che", "El Liberador" and "Viva la Revolución all along the highway coming into town. Now as they travelled down the dusty dirt road that passed for Main Street, there were Che Guevara posters in the market, Che Guevara cups and dinner plates, Che Guevara backpacks and towels.

"You remember that Che was disgusted by what he felt was Fidel Castro's betrayal of the Cuban Revolution, and how he thought that Fidel was turning Cuba into a bureaucratic totalitarian state? So Che left Cuba, ostensibly with Castro's blessing, to carry the socialist revolution to the south. Actually Castro probably just wanted to get rid of him; Che's idealism was becoming a bit of an annoyance.

"When Che arrived in Bolivia he tried to organize the peasants to rebel against the military dictatorship of René Barrientos Ortuño. But he had only a handful of men, no support from Castro, no real local organization, no supply line. He was soon isolated in the hinterlands and then surrounded by CIA-trained Bolivian troops. His men were easily dispatched and Che himself was captured. In short, the so-called Bolivian Revolution failed.

"Che was taken to a nearby schoolroom at La Higuera, very close to here. He was emaciated, suffering from malnutrition, arthritis and chronic asthma. He was tortured for several hours and then shot. That night his hands were cut off to prevent identification, and he was buried beneath the Villagrande airstrip. The military dictator wished to prevent anyone using Che's grave as a place of homage or inspiration for future revolutions.

"His body has since been exhumed and is now in a place of honor in Cuba. But here is where he died and it has been a place of pilgrimage since 1967. In fact, the government is widening the road here, putting in sewerage and electricity. Some entrepreneurs from Santa Cruz are investing heavily in expanding tourist facilities as well. By next year this area will have guest cottages, restaurants, bars, a disco, a museum and much classier Che memorabilia shops to replace the stands in the marketplace."

"Amazing," Teresa said.

"Yes. A socialist revolution is simply another commodity for the capitalists. Of course, this one is safe, since it is a failed revolution that is buried in a history which no one reads. Nowadays Che is simply a fashion statement: a beret, a tee-shirt. And nothing has changed for the people of Bolivia. The peasants are still poor, the indigenous are still abused, and the rich get richer. Except now instead of local exploiters, the global economy is sucking up the natural resources of the country and the sustenance of the people so rapidly it makes everything that went before looks benign by comparison. The Spanish conquistadors were clumsy amateurs compared to this new coalition of corporate conquerors."

CHAPTER TWENTY-TWO

"Hi, Hon. What's the news from Santa Cruz?"

"Hi , Gary. Hey, that rhymes. News from Santa Cruz. Have you been working on your poetry in between tennis matches?"

"Ouch! You go right for the jugular, hey? No, actually I haven't had time for either one. I'm mostly trying to fill in the gaps in the police investigation. Oh, and I'm also sponsoring a really sweet old guy at AA meetings."

He explained about Tommy and how they had become friends in the past few days. He also described how Tommy had discovered a piece of key evidence, and how Gary had invited him to stay in the apartment until he got through the first few difficult days of sobriety. "What's happening at your end?"

"Well, the good news is that your dad left you a tidy fortune in CITCO stocks, about one point four million at today's prices and they're going higher even as we speak."

"Wow!" Gary said, more than a bit stunned. "So, what's the bad news?"

"Well, it seems like your dad's work on micro-economic models put him in conflict with some of the heavy players in agribusiness and land development."

Gary lit a cigarette, and then took the phone and the ash tray out onto the fire escape. He inhaled deeply. Teresa heard the tell-tale sound of the deep inhalation over the phone.

"Don't tell me you're smoking again?" she asked.

"Yeah, an occasional one now and then." He quickly changed the subject to avoid her no-smoking lecture. "So did these developers make threats? Was there anyone with connections to Newport?"

"I don't think so. There aren't any Guatemalans in Newport, are there?"

"Guatemalans!" Gary almost shouted into the phone. "As a matter of fact there are." He went on to explain the discovery of the fishing rod and how Pete McGuire connected the fingerprints to the Guatemalan teen, who received asylum and then died under suspicious circumstances at Fort Adams.

"Well, that might be the connection. One of the big land developers down here uses Guatemalans for security. They're an effective tool to keep the indigenous people in what is essentially a form of slave labor. The Indians work on these enormous plantations in reconverted national forests. The Guatemalans are mostly hardened gang members; they're hired guns who not only keep the Indians in line but also scare off the environmentalists and other investigators."

"So you think this kid may have been a part of that?" Gary asked.

"I think it's pretty likely. You should let Pete McGuire know. The gang might have had some hold on the kid or his family, and that was the price they extracted. Then, after he did his job, they eliminated him."

"These land developers that contracted to hire the Guatemalans. Did you get any names of particular individuals?" Gary asked.

"No. My connections are a law professor, Carlos Rivera, and your father's research assistant, Emma Lee. These are university people who have little actual experience in the field. They didn't know any actual names. Although Emma did see an enforcer who had a tattoo on his arm. It said 'M-13'. She looked it up on the Internet and it refers to a very powerful Central American gang called the Mara Salvatrucha which is known for extortion and murder."

Teresa gave Gary her Continental flight schedule: Santa Cruz to Lima, Lima to Miami, Miami to Newark, Newark to Providence, and assured him that they'd be together in two more days. Before she hung up, however, she cautioned him:

"I don't want to be insensitive and I know how much working with others is a help to your own stability in recovery. And I really do understand the importance of what you're doing," she said. "But I'm assuming this guy's a lot less fragile now that he's detoxed a bit and has a few meetings under his belt. I really do expect that he'll be gone when I get there and we'll have the apartment to ourselves. All right?"

"All right, mi amor. Of course," he replied, hoping that Tommy would understand.

When he hung up he called Pete McGuire at the police station and gave him Teresa's news. "You know," he added, "I didn't even know there were any Guatemalans in Rhode Island."

"Oh, yes indeed," Pete replied. "Quite a few in fact. After we found the kid's body out at Fort Adams, I called a woman by the name of Marta Martínez, at the state historical society. She's a major source on the flow of immigrant groups in Rhode Island. According to her, many of them came as refugees during the civil war when the CIA overthrew the socialist government of Jacobo Arbenz. About 400,000 Guatemalans were killed and another 250,000 fled the military death squads. Many of them were helped by the Catholic Church's sanctuary movement. Then there was a Family Unification bill passed by Congress which brought others up legitimately. There are quite a few Guatemalans on Aquidneck Island now, mostly in Middletown and Portsmouth working in nurseries and owning their own lawn care businesses."

"How does Juan Manuel Andrade fit in with all of that?"

"Well, evidently young Andrade was pressured to join one of the two gangs which now dominate Guatemala City. One is the Mara Salvatrucha or M-13 which was originally a murderous Salvadoran gang; the other, known as M-18, is equally vicious but smaller. Both were actually formed in the California prison system and exported to Central America when the U.S. deported illegal Guatemalans and El Salvadorans back to their homelands."

"Reminds me of a Mexican pun," Gary couldn't help saying. "*De Guatemala a Guatepeor*. From bad to worse."

"That's about it. Anyway, the police can't handle them; the army can't handle them. According to the transcript at Andrade's deportation hearing, he was being pressured by both gangs and had been beat up several times for refusing to join. He was also set upon by one of the 'social cleansing' death squads which assumed he was a gang member because of his age and the barrio where he lived. He barely escaped getting killed, managed to reach Mexico and then crossed the border at Brownsville where he was picked up. As soon as he was in custody, he asked for asylum."

"Which he got because...."

"Well, he had a relative here in Newport. He also had a decent lawyer and support from someone with connections."

"Do you know who that 'connected' person was? It might give us an idea of who's pulling the strings."

126

Pete was quiet for a moment. "I've asked for a transcript of the hearing and I hope to be receiving it shortly. I'll keep you informed. We know that he had a confirmed job, by the way. He was working with a tree care company in Middletown. We're looking into that as well. It's a small company, family-owned; they seem legitimate but are very closed-mouthed. We've looked over their records and their client base. I was able to confirm that your aunt Victoria has a standing contract with them, which is what could have brought Andrade into town, and given him access to the Cliff Walk and to your father."

"I spoke with a Brigadier General Domínguez at the burial. He's attending a summer program the War College on leave from Bolivia. He told me that he thought there was a Bolivian national on the island as well. A fellow by the name of Cesar Castillo. Do you have anything on him?"

"I'll check on that. What else did your Bolivian general tell you?"

"That this Castillo worked for a big land developer in Santa Cruz, one who my father was very critical of in the press and at government hearings."

"And his reason for being in Newport?"

"No idea. The general was positive he had seen him in a shop on Thames Street last week but he disappeared in a crowd near the ferry landing before the general could get to him."

"Okay," Pete replied. "Let me check this out and I'll get back to you sometime tomorrow."

Gary hung up the phone and thought about all he had learned. He knew who his father's killer was. A young Guatemalan kid with no real motive, who was either hired or pressured into committing a crime. And the kid had paid for it with his own life. He also knew that there was a Bolivian involved but he appeared to be a mid-level capo, another pawn, not the brains behind this conspiracy.

Something about the conversation with McGuire struck him as odd. McGuire knew a great deal about the Andrade asylum hearing. He knew that Pilar had offered Andrade a place to live. He knew the name of the company which offered him a job in Middletown. He even knew that Victoria's real estate business was one of its clients. Clearly, McGuire had already seen the transcript of the hearing; he would have accessed that document almost immediately. Therefore, he also knew who Andrade's sponsor was. He knew who had the connections to put weight behind the asylum petition. He called McGuire back.

"Pete, it was the Governor, wasn't it?"

"What are you talking about?"

"You've already seen the transcript of the asylum hearing. The person who sponsored Juan Miguel was the Governor, wasn't it?"

"Gary, I appreciate your help in all of this. You've done a great job collecting evidence. We know who killed your dad and can put 'case closed' to the murder. Now, why don't you let me get on with my part of the investigation and I'll wrap it up. This is police business."

"God damn it, Pete. Why are you playing this game? You know that there's more to this than some Guatemalan kid. You know that this is some kind of conspiracy, and that the Guatemalan kid was just a tool. Don't you want to get to the bottom of it all?"

"Gary. Gary. Don't talk bullshit! Of course, I want to get to the bottom of it," he shouted. Then he paused to get himself under control and spoke more quietly. "Listen. All right? Yes, I *do* know who testified in the asylum case. And, no, it was not the Governor. It was your grandmother. There. Are you happy now? I already questioned her about it. She said that she wanted to help Pilar get her little cousin to safety. So, if you're right and it is some kind of conspiracy, then Pilar is part of it, your grandmother is part of it. Don't you see that you're too close to all of this now? It's time to sit back and let the police take over."

"Yeah. Fine job you've all done so far," Gary said sarcastically. "No, Pete. I'm not backing off now. I'm not leaving until I find out who's really behind it."

CHAPTER TWENTY-THREE

"I'm sorry, Tommy," Gary told him. "But Teresa is arriving in two days and we really need our privacy, you understand. We need our time alone together."

Tommy swallowed his fear. The fear of being on his own again, of not having the support of a sponsor, a companion, a friend living with him. He had been sober now for seventy-two hours. Three days. He'd hoped he would have at least a week's grace before having to fend for himself again. He didn't know if he could make it, but he put on a brave face.

"Sure, Gary. No problem; I understand. I'll be out of here by the end of the day to give you time to clean up the place and get it ready for your wife."

"No, no, Tommy," Gary said, trying to soften the blow. "Listen, tomorrow is fine. Stay here tonight. If you want we can hit another meeting. It's just that I have to see my grandmother and talk to her this afternoon, so if I don't get back in time, you go on ahead and I'll meet you there."

Tommy nodded. He went into the bedroom and got the black plastic garbage bag he had stuffed into one of the drawers. *Might as well go on a scavenging hike, since it's obvious Gary has too much on his mind.* He would have liked to have gone over a couple of the Steps in AA, maybe talk about how he was feeling. But he should have known better than to depend on Gary, or on anyone for that matter. He told Gary he was going for a walk, and headed out the door.

"Take care, buddy," Gary called as Tommy walked down the stairs. "I'll try to catch up with you at the meeting tonight."

Yeah, *buddy*, thought Tommy. You'll *try*. Whenever people said they'd try, he knew it meant that they really didn't believe they'd do it. Like all the times he *tried* to stop drinking. You either stopped or you didn't. Well, he had stopped for three days so far. That proved that he could do it. But keeping it up, what was the point? It was eight more days until he got his veteran's check, and he had only two dollars in his pocket. He'd better start beating the bushes, searching the dumpsters for anything he could turn into cash.

He crossed the gravel path through campus that took him from Ruggles Avenue to Victoria. He passed an apple tree on his left that was bearing fruit. The apples were small, green and hard but might come in handy if he got hungry in the days ahead. He climbed over the short fence, gathered a dozen and put them in his bag.

When he looked across the soccer field he spotted a dead oak which had been uprooted in last night's storm. Next to it was one of those contraptions that shredded the wood. What was it called? A wood chipper. In the old days they would have had men out there with axes and saws to cut the wood into logs for fireplaces and wood stoves. Nowadays wood burning was outlawed by city ordinance to avoid air pollution. He noticed a chunky Latino filling the gas tank of the wood chipper. The guy looked up as Tommy passed and threw him a look of pure contempt. Tommy shivered and looked away. *Yeah well, screw you too, amigo.*

He crossed over to Sheppard Avenue where they had the "monkey seat," an oddity that always amused him on his walks. It was on the back side of the estate called Chateau sur Mer, a place where he had played as a child. The iron chair, which towered above the road, was built for the children of the estate over a hundred years ago. You got up there by climbing a stone wall and then a series of steps hidden among the leaves. It was a great lookout. Just for the hell of it he decided to climb up.

He was half out of breath when he got to the top, although it was not a strenuous climb. A ten year-old kid could do it easily, but it used muscles that grown men didn't ordinarily call upon.

He was about to settle back in the chair, perched high above the roadway, when he noticed the edge of a plastic bag sticking out of a crevice in the stone wall below him. He put his cigarette back in the pack and descended the stairs. Cautiously he eased himself down over the iron bars onto the stone wall. He slid down off the wall and, protected from anyone's view on the road, pulled the plastic bag out from the cleft in the rock. It was a bag full of peach-colored pills. Maybe a couple thousand of them. He recognized them immediately. OxyContin. A heroin substitute. He knew that he could probably get ten dollars per tablet from just about anyone that wanted to get high. That would solve his financial problems. *Say, two thousand at ten bucks each. Nice piece of change.*

But then he thought about recovery. About how honesty was probably his only real hope of staying clean and sober. Plus, there was something evil in getting clean yourself and then selling the poison to someone else. He decided to open the plastic bag, dump the contents on the side of the road and then crush the capsules under foot until they were dust that the wind would blow away. That would take care of the problem. He put the bag on the top of the wall and then eased himself over to the other side. His joints were creaky these days and getting over these old stone walls was more of a chore than he remembered.

He had just turned the bag over to dump the contents when two Harleys came roaring up the road. One braked right in front of him and the other cut behind him, both engines roaring with menace. He was surrounded, cut off, and *in flagrante delicto* with a sack containing $20,000 worth of pills in his hand.

The riders both wore Levis, leather vests, and patches which read '1%', indicating that they were outlaw bikers. The one in front of him had a Devil's Disciples decal on his vest, long stringy hair, and weighed in at about three hundred pounds. He looked like a pro wrestler, bulky but with hardness to the fat. His partner, who had maneuvered his bike behind Tommy, was tall and lanky with a Ho Chi Ming beard, wispy and greasy. The wrestler-type gave him a pleasant grin and asked, "What have you got there, brother? That there bag looks suspiciously like our property."

Tommy felt his sphincter muscle tighten. He was afraid. No, more than that. He was scared to death. There was no one around. He had a sack of pills worth twenty thousand dollars, and these guys would not take it lightly that he appeared to be ripping off their stash. They could simply beat him to death, toss him over the wall, and be off—back to East Providence or whatever hole they had crawled out of.

"I'll take that bag you're carrying, punk," ordered the Ho Chi Ming biker, pulling a gun from beneath his belt and pointing it at Tommy.

Tommy handed it over and as he did so, the heavy biker struck him a sucker blow to the head. He went down in a heap and both bikers turned off their engines, put the kickstands down, and slowly approached. He closed his eyes as one of them reared back to kick him in the ribs. Then, suddenly, there was the whoop-whoop of a police siren, and a squad car came flying across the street, slamming into both of the Harleys before skidding to a stop

Officer Rego, who had been parked in the driveway across the street hidden by a grove of trees, had his Sig Sauer automatic out and covered both bikers efficiently. "Drop your weapon now!" he ordered Ho Chi Ming. "And both of you, on your knees! Right now, move it!"

He tossed a set of handcuffs to Tommy. "Give me a little help, Sullivan, and put these cuffs on fatso over there."

When the big biker was cuffed, Rego pushed him face down on the pavement and then tossed a second set of restraints over to Tommy. "Cuff him now, while I cover them both."

Tommy complied, hands shaking as he ratcheted the cuffs around each wrist. When he finished he looked up. Rego had retrieved a .38 police special and a set of brass knuckles as well as a baggie which appeared to contain cocaine. He put all the items on the hood of his squad car. Then he pushed the second suspect facedown on the roadway. "Stay there, dude, and don't move an inch."

"I called for backup," he said, turning to Tommy. "About ten minutes ago. They should be here any second. "Tommy could, in fact, already hear the sirens in the distance. "But I figured if I didn't act before they got here, you would have had one hell of a beating."

"Thanks, Rego."

"Ah, no big deal. As a matter of fact, you've done me a favor. Now, I've got these asswipes for aggravated assault and battery with a deadly weapon, as well as possession of narcotics for sale. We'll put them away for a long time."

Tommy looked at him and, unbelievably, Rego was smiling at him in a friendly way. "Besides all that," he added quietly, "you're the first street person on my beat who's staying sober in AA. So that's one less shopping cart I'll have to chase down and return to the Stop and Shop."

Two minutes later three more police cars arrived including one with the supervising lieutenant, then an unmarked DEA vehicle, and a paramedic unit from the Newport Fire Department. Uniformed police took the two bikers into custody while Rego radioed in for a tow truck to pick up the Harleys. The DEA agent and the supervisor had a little discussion over that and then the lieutenant came over to where Rego and Tommy were standing. Tommy was having his head wound cleaned and dressed by one of the medics.

"Would you believe that DEA jerk?" he said to Rego. "He wants to confiscate the Harleys as part of his operation. I told him no way, José, my officer made the bust and those Harleys are now the property of the City of Newport. Damn feds. They think they can just step in and take what they want, when they want." He looked over at Tommy. "And how are you doing there, Sullivan?"

"I'm fine," Tommy said. "A little headache is all. I'll be all right."

"Well, we should take you in for observation, just to be sure."

"No, Lieutenant, I don't want to do that!" Tommy protested vehemently. "I really need to get to an AA meeting."

"Well," he said, looking over at Rego. Rego nodded his assent. "Okay, then. After we get your statement, I'm going to have Officer Rego drive you to your meeting. If you feel dizzy or nauseous at any time, I want you to call him. Clem, give him your card. Sergeant Crowley, get over here and take their statements."

A young red-headed sergeant came over and with a clipboard and an incident report form. He nodded for Rego to go ahead, and Rego described how he had seen Tommy searching for discarded cans to recycle. He pointed to Tommy's plastic bag as the sergeant took notes. "Then he came upon the bikers' stash and was about to dump it out, crushing the pills in the street, when the two Harleys arrived. I witnessed the initial assault and the battery, and then determined that if I waited for backup the witness would be seriously injured, even killed."

Tommy was amazed. Rego saved his ass. How could he have guessed Tommy was going to destroy the pills? The biker came up on him with the bag still in his hands. But he wasn't going to blow it. Confirming Rego's account of the events, he completed his statement to the sergeant and again to the DEA agent, then finally to a county narcotics detective and a DEA supervisor who came just as he was finishing up.

"Okay," Rego said. "That's it. If you guys want any more just check each other's notes. Tommy, you go ahead and get in my car."

"Front seat or back?" Tommy asked suspiciously, wondering whether the cops weren't still considering him to be at least marginally involved in some criminal activity.

Rego smiled. "Front seat, Tommy. Don't worry. We'll go up to the Newport Creamery and then I'll drive you over to your meeting. Right now you're looking like you could use a little refreshment. I know I sure could."

Rego drove them to the Bellevue Shopping Center, calling into the station to let them know he'd be out of service for the next thirty minutes. He parked the car and they walked to the Creamery where he treated Tommy and himself to two "Awful, Awfuls", double-rich chocolate milk shakes.

"The best thing in the world when you've been in a situation like ours," Rego said. "We always used to drink these after football games when I was in high school. They make up for the sugar loss from the adrenaline rush, coat your stomach, and also put some vitamin D and some calcium into your system. Much better than alcohol. Although, if you're like me, a drink is probably the first thing you wanted."

Tommy looked up from his milkshake. "How did you...."

"I'm a "friend of Bill" and all that, too. I just don't go to meetings here in town. I had some trouble with resentments, still do. After my dad died, I hit the sauce a bit too hard, so I decided I'd get some help with it. Not everyone understands, and some lowlifes would love to put me in a bind if they knew I was in recovery. A cop in a small town is pretty vulnerable."

"Well," said Tommy. "It's an anonymous program. No one will ever hear it from me. What's said between us will stay between us. Speaking of which....I have a confession to make. When I first found those pills I thought about taking them and selling them. But then I changed my mind. I realized that I couldn't do that and stay sober. The guilt would get to me and I'd start drinking again."

"Well, like you said, Tommy, what's between us stays between us. Plus, there's no law against thinking. It's what you finally do that determines who you are and what your character is. You did the right thing. Come on; let's head over to that meeting."

He drove down Bellevue using the flashing lights this time because the meeting would start in five minutes and he didn't want Tommy to be late. He turned off the flashers as they turned into the street so as not to alarm anyone. As he pulled up to the meeting house, he reminded Tommy to call him if he had any headache or nausea.

"No problem," Tommy said. "Sure you don't want to join me?"

"No thanks," Rego said. "Newport might be getting more liberal, but it's still not ready for uniformed cops at AA meetings. I'll see you around."

"Um, Officer Rego?"

"Call me Clem," Rego smiled, shaking Tommy's hand and then putting the car into gear. "Take care now, Tommy."

"Um…Clem. Hold up a second. There's just one more thing. It might not mean anything and then again it might. When I was walking through the campus on the gravel path that leads from Ruggles to Sheppard, I saw this fat Latino guy fooling around with a wood chipper."

"So? Nothing strange about that. Lots of branches down from last night's storm, and several of these tree companies employ Latinos."

"I know. I know. But something about this guy. Chunky, not muscle, but hard fat. A foreman type. Anyway, he looked at me like he hated my guts."

"Does this have something to do with Professor Regan's death and that investigation, do you think?"

"I don't know. I just feel that…well, to survive on the streets you need good instincts. You need to know who's likely to hurt you and who's harmless. This guy looked like he'd enjoy hurting someone."

"Okay, Tommy. I'll keep my eye out. Call me, if you need to. You've got my card."

Rego pulled away and headed back up to Bellevue. *Paranoid, most likely. Hanging around with Regan's son probably has him seeing Latino killers lurking behind every tree.*

Just minutes after he made the turn onto Broadway, he had a call for a domestic dispute out at Park Holm. As he adjusted his belt and loosened the nightstick in its holder, he put Tommy and his suspicions out of his mind. There were more immediate concerns.

CHAPTER TWENTY-FOUR

When Gary arrived at his grandmother's house, he noticed the Governor's car in the driveway and a police car parked in front of the large maple tree at the curb. He hurried to the front door where he was met by the Governor.

"Your grandmother is in intensive care at Newport Hospital," he said as Gary came into the house. Although his eyes expressed sorrow, his face was composed and his Armani suit was freshly-pressed. "She had a stroke when she heard about the death of Juan Miguel. Perhaps she blamed herself, since she was instrumental in getting him to settle here. At any rate, she's in critical condition. I intend to head to the hospital as soon as I finish answering questions for Detective McGuire."

Gary looked behind him and saw McGuire and a uniformed cop in the living room.

"Please, come in, Gary, and sit down for a minute," the Governor offered.

Gary entered the book-lined living room, and helped himself to a glass of lemonade from a tray on the sideboard that held an iced pitcher. He shook hands with McGuire and the uniformed cop who introduced himself as Officer Tyler.

"And Pilar?" Gary asked. "Was she involved in this somehow?"

"We don't think so," McGuire said. "She's upstairs. The doctor gave her a sedative. She was totally distraught when she heard what happened. She blames herself, not only for her cousin's death, but also for your grandmother's stroke. As far as we can determine, Pilar had nothing to do with any of it. The cousin became involved with some lowlife. Pilar had seen him talking to someone she described as...." He consulted his notes. "A chunky, heavy-set man in his forties. Although Latino, he did not appear to be Guatemalan. She thought maybe South American. At any rate, shortly after Pilar saw Juan Miguel with this man, the boy became secretive and nervous, like he was involved in something. A few days later he was dead."

Gary turned to the Governor. "And what's your part in all this? I know you're not an innocent bystander."

The Governor shook his head. "I know little more than you do, Gary. I know that your grandmother felt she was doing Pilar a favor, stepping up and sponsoring the cousin."

He spoke sincerely, Gary thought, but that probably came from long years of experience as a politician. *He probably always sounds sincere, even when he's lying through his teeth.*

"And how about my father's coming to Newport? How about the Bolivian general conveniently attending a conference at the Naval War College? Are you going to tell me that someone as influential as yourself, someone who is so attuned to every nuance of life in Newport...that you were unaware and had no part in those developments either?"

The Governor turned his back on Gary and leaned over to McGuire. "Is Gary one of your official interrogators? I don't mind answering questions, but I feel like I should draw a line here between what is officially required, and what is just a matter of idle curiosity."

"Idle curiosity? You son-of-a-bitch! Don't turn your back on me!" Gary shouted. "There have been at least two murders in the past week; one of them was my father. My grandmother has had a stroke. And you, conveniently, seem to be on the sidelines, untouched. My father who taught at a university in Bolivia, a Bolivian general, and a South America national—probably another Bolivian for all I know—were all in Newport at the same time. Don't pretend you know nothing about it!"

"Gary, Gary. Hold up a minute," McGuire ordered. "I questioned the Governor about your father's invitation to be part of the globalization conference at the Pell Center. Apparently that was a decision made by Dr. Alioto, although the Governor was consulted. Your father had evidently applied for a fellowship in the past, to work on a book about Latin American views on globalization. It was determined that this was not an appropriate use of the facilities, given your father's leftist leanings, so the offer to take part in the conference was seen by both Dr. Alioto and the Governor as an acceptable compromise. Your father would be invited to participate but his ideas would be subject to criticism and scrutiny by other scholars."

"And the Bolivian general? How does he explain him?"

"Let me answer that, Pete," the Governor interjected. "I had been asked by some people I know in the corporate world if I would support the general's attendance at a conference on continental security initiatives. Bolivia is one of the key players in the hemisphere and one that we especially want to encourage, since it can counterbalance the saber-rattling of Chávez and his minions in Venezuela."

"Who are these people in the corporate world? What is their interest? They wouldn't happen to be biofuel companies or agribusiness conglomerates that the general was investigating, would they?"

"I was aware of no such investigations,"the Governor replied indignantly.

"Then you admit that the request came from one of these...."

"I admit nothing," the Governor interrupted. "I did absolutely nothing wrong!"

"Okay, okay!" McGuire interrupted. "Everyone settle down. Gary, you had better leave the questioning to me. I'll keep you informed if we find out anything else that connects these events to your father's death. In the meantime, you might want to get back over to the university and catch up with your friend Tommy Sullivan. He had a bit of a tussle this afternoon with some bikers and got knocked around a little bit."

"Is he okay?"

"Yes, he appears to be. Officer Rego dropped him off at an AA meeting on campus. He said you'd know where he was. So, listen. Go check on him. Then give the hospital a call when the meeting is over and get an update on your grandmother's condition. I'll follow up on the Bolivians and I'll keep you up to date. If I find anything relevant to your father's death, I'll let you know. Okay?"

Gary turned to the Governor and gave him a warning look. "I guess it will have to be okay," Gary said. "For now. But don't let this slick talker off the hook. He knows something and he's involved in it somehow. He's up to his neck in corporate manipulations and political shenanigans. Probably has been all his sorry life. Only this time people are dying as a result."

Gary slammed out the door, got on his bike and pedaled down Harrison, across Old Fort Road, then down Carroll to the top of the Ruggles hill. He was going at a fast clip when he hit the crest of the hill so he let the bike coast and enjoyed the speed, the wind in his face and the reckless speed. He was aware that he was going a bit too fast, but there was no traffic on the road and no real danger. There were no ruts and the road was well-maintained.

Suddenly, he heard the rush of a motor and saw a streak of green as a pickup truck brushed the rear fender of his bike and the bike went out of control, flew off the road and crashed into a ditch. He was flung head first over the handlebars and would have slammed into a tree had not his body twisted to land him in a pile of leaves that had been deposited there by a homeowner violating the law against roadside dumping. He was bruised and shaken, but seeing how close he had come to mortal injury, he felt blessed. A couple of inches to the right and he would have joined his father and Juan Miguel in the morgue.

He brushed himself off, tested his still-shaking legs, and then straightened his bike, which was scratched but basically undamaged by the crash. He got back on and pedaled painfully up the other side of Ruggles. He stopped at Bellevue to catch his breath and let a long stream of cars pass him headed for the music festival at Fort Adams. When he saw a gap in the traffic, he walked the bike across Bellevue, then remounted and rode down to Ochre Point Road. He made it to the meeting in less than fifteen minutes, sweating, driven by adrenaline. However, when he got there he had to restrain himself. The meeting had already begun. He took a seat in the rear and looked around for his friend.

Tommy was sitting in one of the front rows. He had a bandage on his scalp and another over his left ear, but he turned around and gave Gary the thumbs up sign. Gary shot back a quizzical nod in his direction but it went unanswered. He only half-paid attention during the meeting; he was too caught up in the mystery of the Governor's possible involvement in his father's death. Now he had the new problem of Tommy and his latest trauma, and Teresa would be arriving shortly. How could he kick Tommy out of the apartment now that he was injured? The answer was…he couldn't. He would let him stay at the apartment at least until he had a whole week of sobriety. He hoped Teresa would understand, but he just couldn't send Tommy back onto the streets.

Then he began to think of his own accident. It was unusual in Newport for a motorist not to stop and give aid when there was an accident; it was also, of course, against the law to drive off. There was the possibility that the motorist did not realize he'd hit the bike, and hadn't looked into the rearview mirror. But that, too, was strange. In Newport, as in most small New England towns, drivers usually gave bicyclists a wide berth because they knew how vulnerable bikes were on the roadways. But this guy had not moved over at all, even with the other lane empty and no another cars around. Could it have been done on purpose? Gary had not seen the driver. He seemed to remember the truck as an older model pickup. Unwashed, Kelly green, something that a landscaper might drive.

CHAPTER TWENTY-FIVE

On the way home from the meeting Gary listened to Tommy's tale of dope and bikers with sympathetic amazement. He was grateful to Rego for saving Tommy's life, but he was puzzled by what followed. He found it hard to understand why Rego would offer an alibi to the police about Tommy searching for the cans and intending to destroy the pills. Even more incredible, why he would treat Tommy to an Awful-Awful at the Creamery, and chauffeur him to an AA meeting. It was all a bit much. He was suspicious of Rego's motivations. When he tried to get Tommy to explain how he and Rego had become so close, Tommy—true to his promise to respect the policeman's anonymity—refused to go into any details. When Gary pressed for more, Tommy became annoyed, so Gary let it go.

"Tommy, I've thought over what I told you about moving out of the apartment. I think that now is not such a good time. When Teresa arrives I'll explain it to her, but right now, I just want you to move your stuff to the bedroom on the top floor. Then I'll make us some coffee, and clean up the lower bedroom for Teresa and me.

Tommy brightened visibly. "You mean, I don't have to move out?" I can really stay?"

"That's right, Tommy."

"And your wife, what will she...."

"Don't worry about Teresa. She's a good person. We'll work it out."

Night had descended as they walked home together, Tommy swinging his arms, Gary hampered by the banged-up bicycle that he pushed along beside him. Except for an occasional wispy cloud, the sky was clear with all the stars visible because they were far enough from downtown and its light pollution. Tommy, enlivened by the news that he still had a safe place to stay, began regaling Gary with the names of constellations and the stars which composed them. He pointed out Orion's belt and sword, Polaris, the red giant Betelgeuse and then Sirius. When Gary asked about the twinkling bright star to the west, Gary told him that it was the sign that Gary and Teresa would soon be together.

"What do you mean? What star is that, anyway?" Gary asked.

"It's not a star at all," Tommy told him with a smile. "It's the planet Venus."

When they arrived back at the apartment, Dr. Alioto was waiting in his Taurus, parked in the back lot. He powered down the window and greeted them.

"I came to see you earlier, but when I got no answer I figured you must be out for a bike ride." He eyed the dented bicycle which he'd loaned Gary a few days ago in pristine condition, and sighed deeply. Gary pushed it over to the side and leaned it up against the building.

"It looks a little banged up," Alioto observed.

"I'm sorry, Paul. Some jerk ran me off the road earlier today as I was coming down the Ruggles' hill. Damn near killed me. But I'll get it fixed up and painted before I return it."

"Don't worry about that," Alioto said. "Are you okay? That's the important thing."

"Yes, I'm fine. A little bruised and I'll be sore in the morning, but no broken bones." He turned to Tommy. "By the way, this is my friend Tommy Sullivan. I don't believe you two have met."

Tommy and Dr. Alioto shook hands, and then Alioto returned his attention to Gary.

"Well, listen. I was wondering if you'd like to go get a cup of coffee? I received a call from the Governor and he said you were very upset. Also, that you were disturbed by the odd combination of factors that brought your father to the conference here. I thought I might be able to explain a bit about that."

"Sure," Gary said. "Coffee would be great. But we don't need to go out. Tommy has some things to do upstairs. Why don't I make some coffee in the kitchen and you can fill me in?"

They went inside and Tommy made them all coffee. Then he retreated to the upstairs bedroom while Gary and Alioto settled into the living room.

"Well," Alioto observed. "It all started several years ago when we began offering competitive fellowships to international scholars who wished to come to the Pell Center and work on projects that would have a global impact. Your father submitted a proposal which made our short list. It was fairly complex. It involved a micro-economic model in Bolivia which had implications for development around the world. The study itself was relatively benign. It was a study, that's all.

"The implications of the study were the problem. Your father's believed that it would show the failure of global capitalism and the ultimate destruction of entire economies, ecosystems and cultures. We ultimately found these conclusions unacceptable. He also extrapolated the results to show that current capitalist models would result in less freedom and less democracy around the world within a decade."

"Who was the *we* that you're referring to?" Gary asked.

"The review panel. It was composed of a number of scholars from various disciplines such as economics, sociology and political science. Anyway, your father submitted the same proposal, with a few minor changes, the following year. This time he had letters of recommendation from various scholars who supported his thesis. They were mostly, as Professor Bergman from Boston University would say, "leftist intellectuals from across the River." They included Berkowitz from Harvard and Chomsky from MIT. People, I should add, that most mainstream economists do not take seriously."

"Because mainstream economists are wedded to the sort of global capitalist model that my father criticized?"

"Be that as it may," Alioto replied with just a hint of annoyance. Clearly he was used to holding forth with students, uninterrupted. "The panel rejected his second application," he continued. "*The panel*, you understand, not any one individual. Your father, however, was convinced that the Governor and his friends were behind it. He felt that the Governor was in bed, so to speak, with multinational corporations, the Department of Defense, and the Republican Party. He believed that the Governor had taken steps to ensure that he would never be allowed to air his views in this academic setting."

"So, what happened?"

"Well, I know that there were several letters between your father and the Governor. A couple of those the Governor shared with me. He was concerned. After all, your father was a noted scholar. He was also a Newport native. The proposal was a good one, but so were several of the others for which we finally granted fellowships. At any rate, the Governor proposed a compromise. He suggested that I invite your father as a participant in the conference on globalization this summer. That would give him a chance to air his views, and to have them tested, as it were, in an adversarial fashion. It would also give those in residence at the Center an opportunity to finally dismiss his conclusions, since your father would be a lone anti-globalist with no real allies in the group. To the rest of the world, it would appear that we were being open-minded and generous."

"My father agreed to this?" Gary asked.

"Yes, he did. He was not particularly happy with the agreement. And, as it turned out, he had many unpleasant confrontations, especially with Professor Bergman, during the short time he was here. But you already know about that. The point I want to make is that there was nothing sinister about the invitation."

"But why did the Governor propose the compromise?" Gary asked. "Why didn't he just ignore the letters? And you're the director of the Center. If you didn't agree, why did you go along with it?"

Alioto blushed and for a moment seemed at a loss for words. Then he collected himself. "Well, that's a fair question. Let me try to answer as best I can…. As to why the Governor just didn't ignore the letters, well—I always felt that there was some unfinished business between Michael and the Governor. I'm not sure what it was but somehow the Governor always seemed a bit guilty about something in the past involving your father." He paused for just a moment. "I don't suppose you would know anything about that?"

"No," Gary lied. "I have no idea. But then I wouldn't know anything much. My father and I haven't been in touch for years."

"Well. The second question was why did I go along with it? That's a bit more straightforward, but still convoluted to a non-academic, I'm afraid. The Pell Center was founded by Senator

Claiborne Pell, a Democrat and a liberal. Your father had mentioned in one of his letters that having so many corporate economists and Republican strategists in residence made a mockery of Senator Pell's mandate for open, multi-partisan discussions of world affairs. Frankly, I agreed with him, although I was powerless to change the Center's focus, since both the Board of Directors and the selection panels had become dominated by conservative professors and by what Eisenhower famously called the 'military-industrial complex'. So, you see my collusion in the decision to have your father come was easily acquired."

Just then the phone rang and he heard Tommy come down the stairs to answer it. He waited a moment.

"It's for you, Gary," Tommy said handing him the phone.

"Gary, it's Pete McGuire. I just got a call from one of my contacts in Homeland Security. It seems your wife has been detained at the Houston airport by customs agents. According to his report, she was travelling on an illegal passport."

"What!"

"I don't have all the details. But I do have a number you can call for Homeland Security to get more information."

After jotting down the number, Gary thanked him and hung up. He was livid with anger and frustration. "God damn sons-of-bitches. Lousy sons-of-bitches! I can't believe this! Teresa has been arrested at the Houston airport by Homeland Security. It seems there's some kind of mix-up with her passport. I've got the number to call them. Bastards! Damn bastards!"

"Gary, settle down," Tommy said, taking the phone away from him and setting it back in its cradle. "You've also got a card in your pocket from Jim Sloan, the attorney we met the other night at the meeting. Have him make the call, find out what's going on, and take the steps that need to be taken. You can't do anything from here, and in your emotional state, you'll only fuck things up."

Alioto looked at Tommy with a new-found respect. "I think your friend is right, Gary. Call a lawyer. In the meantime, if you'd like, I can speak to the Governor. I'm sure he's got some influence with the agency or at least knows someone in Washington who could be helpful."

"Fuck, no! I don't want the Governor's help." Gary caught himself and reined in his temper. "Listen, Paul. Thanks for coming by. I appreciate your being so forthcoming. You've been very helpful. But now if you don't mind, I need to be alone and make some calls. Could you see yourself out?"

When Alioto left, Gary retrieved the card for the lawyer he'd met at the AA meeting, called him on his cell, and explained the problem. Jim Sloan was quietly efficient. He said he would call in to the immigration office at the Houston airport right away and would get back to him as soon as possible. He scheduled a formal meeting with Gary for nine the next morning at his Broadway offices.

"In the meantime, get some rest," he advised. "As soon as I have any news, I'll call you."

Less than an hour later, Sloan called back. "Well, here's the latest. Your wife was travelling on an expired U.S. passport. According to her, she had applied for a passport renewal two months ago but the updated passport had not arrived when she booked her flight to Bolivia. Due to all the delays they've been having with passport renewals lately, they are generally willing to be flexible. If she had a date- stamped receipt proving that she had paid the renewal fee, they might have gone ahead and let her though. But she didn't."

"But she also had a Mexican passport," Gary argued. "She's a dual citizen. Couldn't they accept the other passport?" Gary asked.

"Well, that's where she got into trouble it seems. She did have a Mexican passport. But customs officials frown on people with two passports, even though they are perfectly legal. With Mexicans, or any brown people, it seems this is especially true. If you use the American one and it's up-to-date with at least ninety days remaining on it, you can usually enter the U.S. with no problem. But if you use the Mexican one, you need a visa from the local consul general, in her case, the one in Guadalajara. She didn't obtain that."

"So where is she now? What's happening?"

"She's not in detention. I was able to get her released from the immigration lockup. However, she is currently being held in the International Transit section of the Houston airport. It looks like they are going to make her return to Guadalajara to get proper documentation. However, I've taken the liberty of calling Governor Whitman and seeing if he can pull a few strings. He has connections in the State Department."

"Damn," Gary swore. "I wish you hadn't done that. He's a manipulative son-of-a-bitch and I don't want to owe him any damn favors."

"Well, quite frankly, Gary, I don't believe that's really your call. You hired me to represent Teresa's best interests in this matter, and that is what I'm doing. I think she'd prefer to get released from detention and get a flight to Newport as soon as possible, don't you?"

Gary winced in shame. "Yes, of course, you're right. I've just been having a few issues with the Governor lately. But you're absolutely right. You need to do whatever you can to get Teresa out and back on the plane."

"Okay, then. I'll keep you informed. I doubt there will be any more activity before morning. For now, Teresa is all right. She won't be able to make any calls until this is resolved. But she has a credit card, so she can order food from the restaurant there. She'll be sleeping on one of the plastic chairs in the international waiting area, but many passengers have to do that when their flights are delayed. It'll be uncomfortable, but bearable. If they refuse to let her into the country, which is likely, then she'll have to return to Guadalajara, get a visa, and then fly back."

"Shit! That could take weeks."

"Maybe not. The other possibility is that they could provide her with a duplicate of the receipt for her U.S. passport renewal fee. In either case, the Governor could be very helpful in getting the consulate to expedite the request. As mentioned, he has friends in the State Department."

Gary thanked the lawyer, promised to come by in the morning with his retainer, then hung up. He told Tommy what was going on and then excused himself to have a smoke on the fire escape, and mull over this latest development. He doubted he would get much sleep tonight thinking about Teresa, now huddled up on a hard plastic chair in the international transit section of the Houston airport after her long trip from Bolivia. He could also imagine her frustration and humiliation at being treated like a second class citizen. How had Sloan put it? 'With Mexicans, or any brown people it seems, this is especially true.' Despite the fact that she was married to an American and had full citizenship status, he had witnessed several instances of her being singled out for verbal abuse and contemptible treatment at U.S. airports.

Since 9/11 it had gotten much worse. It appeared to Gary that Homeland Security, along with Lou Dobbs and the rest of the xenophobes on Fox TV, behaved as if anyone: Iraqis, Venezuelans, even Mexicans, were responsible for the attacks on the twin towers instead of Al Qaida. He was reminded of the story of a fellow searching for his lost ring under a streetlight. When a passerby asked him what he was doing, he said that he had lost his ring and was searching for it. "Where did you lose it?" The passerby asked. "Over there," the man said pointing to a dark area of the street.

"Well, if you lost it over there, why are you searching here under the streetlight?"

"Well, isn't it obvious," the man replied. "The light is much better over here!"

We attack those who are easiest to attack, Gary, thought, *while the real culprits roam free.*

CHAPTER TWENTY-SIX

The next morning Gary called a cab and he and Tommy went to the eight a.m meeting at St. Joseph's. At 8:40 Gary left Tommy at the meeting and walked to the offices of James Sloan and Associates on Broadway. Sloan brought him up to date on the passport process, assured him that Teresa was fine and that she was en route to Guadalajara where a State Department driver would meet with her and take her to the consulate. Gary wrote him a check for his retainer, thanked him, and headed over to Newport Hospital. He wanted to spend a little time with his grandmother before he left that part of town.

He checked at the front desk and found that she had been released from intensive care and was in a private room. When he got off the elevator and turned the corner to the room she was assigned, he heard voices, and stopped outside the door. He peeked around the corner. The Governor was sitting close to the bed holding his grandmother's hand. He was murmuring softly to her and, although her face was a bit distorted from the effects of the stroke, it was apparent that his grandmother was smiling. Gary was reluctant to enter. He had mixed feelings about the Governor being there, but he also knew that the two of them had maintained their love over many decades of life and it was apparent that it had not diminished with age.

She caught Gary's eye though, before he could back away, and the Governor, following her gaze, looked up. He seemed a bit nonplussed to be caught in a posture of such intimacy, but he recovered well and invited Gary to come in.

"I was just getting ready to leave, he said smoothly. "Come in and sit for a while with your grandmother."

"No, don't go," the grandmother said, clinging to the Governor's hand. "Gary, come over here and give me a kiss. Then, I need to tell you a few things."

Gary eased over to the bed and kissed her on the cheek. "You don't need to tell me anything, Grandma. Just get some rest. I only came by to see that you were okay and find out if you needed anything."

"I have everything I need, Gary," she said, smiling over at the Governor. "We have been through a great many tragedies together, and they seem to have multiplied over the past few days. 'When sorrows come, they come not single spies but in battalions.' But I want you to know that Governor Whitman is not the one responsible, as you seem to think. Yes, he did some favors for some people, and, yes, favors sometimes do have a way of backfiring. But the most pressing concern you have, the business of the Bolivian general, was actually something your Aunt Victoria, cooked up. It seems she was approached by one of her largest real estate investors to get this general out of the hair of some of his associates in land development back in Bolivia. They put together a proposal for him to come to the War College, and she asked the Governor to push the application through. Frankly, he knew nothing more about it, only that he was doing a favor for my sister."

She lay back against the pillows, exhausted by this lengthy revelation. The Governor wiped her brow with a damp cloth, and then reached for a glass of water by the bedside table. She sipped the water through a straw for a few seconds, crookedly smiling her thanks.

"Now, I'm sure you've got many things to do with your day. If you're still tracking down information, why not go over and speak to Victoria? In the meantime, Gary, I do appreciate your coming by but I really need to rest."

Gary gave her a peck on the cheek, told her he loved her, and then nodded goodbye to the Governor. There was more here than met the eye, he was sure, and the Governor's complicity was still far from disproven. But nothing would be gained by giving either of them the third degree here in the hospital. He decided to take her advice and pay a visit to his aunt's real estate office.

Gary walked up to Spring Street and then down to the real estate office on Memorial Boulevard. He used the time to think about what he would say to his aunt. Like his grandmother, she was elderly but very sharp. She had little love for Gary and had made her way in the world, both financially and socially, by being more astute and more ruthless than her male competitors. He doubted that she would have any remorse when Gary told her that she derailed an investigation in Bolivia which might have helped to save indigenous people in that country from brutality and slavery. But at least it would give him the opportunity to see who was behind the general's timely removal from Santa Cruz, and what role the Governor played.

When he arrived at the offices of Regan and Stein, he could hear the thunk of tennis balls from the Newport Casino back of the parking lot. It seemed like a lifetime since he had last been on a tennis court. He missed it and hoped that when all of this was over, he'd have a chance to play a bit in Newport before the cold weather set in.

He walked through the reception area, past the photos of million-dollar homes on easels. He told Oliver that he was there to see his aunt. The irrepressible secretary nodded his reluctant acquiescence and disappeared into Victoria's office. He reappeared quickly and ushered Gary inside. Victoria came out from behind her ornate Edwardian desk and briskly shook his hand.

"You've just come from seeing your grandmother, I take it?" she asked.

"Yes. She seems to be doing much better," Gary noted.

"Yes, but not well enough to return home, I don't believe. Not now, and perhaps not ever without full time care. But that's not why you're here, I suspect. She told you something about my request to the Governor promote General Domínguez's attendance at the War College seminar? Well, it was straightforward enough. It was a favor for a client who was purchasing a thirty million dollar property. He was CEO of an agribusiness concern. It was a large purchase and, I might add, a large commission. So, I said I'd pull some strings to entice this general up from Bolivia, where he had proven an annoyance to my client's corporation."

"I don't suppose you'd have even a twinge of conscience if I told you that this general was investigating the abuse and forced labor of hundreds of indigenous people at the time and that this diversion may have put those people even more at risk?" Gary asked.

"There you go again," Victoria sneered. "Here comes the self-righteous attack. You are so much like your father. No, Gary, I don't know the specifics of what goes on in Bolivia, nor do I much care. I'm sure if we sat down and analyzed every investment Americans have made over two hundred and fifty years we'd find that we are somehow implicated in everything: slavery, Chinese opium, bootlegging, prostitution, wholesale destruction of the forests. My concern is to please my clients, make a profit and invest wisely. Usually that does not include championing Bolivian peasants and supporting socialists. Now if you'll excuse me, I have work to do."

She turned back to her desk, sat down and began to occupy herself with paperwork. Gary was tempted to lambast her for her cavalier attitude but then thought better of it. It would accomplish nothing. She had got this far in life by being essentially a hidebound sociopath, interested only in her own personal bottom line. She cared little what he thought. In fact, she probably considered him, like the Bolivians, a disposable person.

He walked out of the office and headed back to the packing lot to peek over the fence at the Casino tennis courts where he could still hear the balls in play. As he did so, he glimpsed a green pickup parked behind the real estate offices. A heavy-set Latino, barrel-chested and with a pock-marked face, was loading some gas cans into the back of the truck. Gary walked over and greeted him.

"¿Como está, Senor?" Gary suspected that this was the Bolivian who had employed Juan Manuel, but he didn't want to jump to conclusions. He didn't want to so easily join the ranks of those 'racial profiling' types who just assumed that being Latino meant being up to no good.

The man nodded. "Aquí, no más," he said stoically.

"Disculpe, Señor. ¿Usted trabaja por Señorita Victoria?"

"Yes, I work for the Señora," he replied in English. "I cut trees, do lawn work, plant flower beds.
It is all for a business she contracts in Middletown."

"Ah, this must be one of those successful Guatemalan concerns that I've heard some much about. Tell me did a young man by the name of Juan Manuel Andrade work for your company as well?

"Yes, I knew Juan Manuel. He came to an unfortunate end."

"And where are you from in Guatemala?"

"*¿Y por que tantas preguntas?*" the Latino asked. "What are you after, my nosy friend?" He leaned over the side of the truck and produced a pistol from under the tarp. "Perhaps you'd better turn around."

As Gary turned, the man clipped him on the back of the head with his pistol. Gary was stunned, and staggered to the side of the pickup. Then he was hit again, this time with the butt against his temple: he felt as if his head was split wide open and collapsed against the side of the pickup.

When he awoke his head was throbbing and he was bound with rope in the back of the truck which was thumping along uneven terrain. He smelled gasoline from the cans in the truck bed, as well as the sweet odor of wood chips and sawdust. Suddenly the pickup came to an abrupt stop.

He heard the front door open and the driver get out. Then he heard an auxiliary engine starting up, the clanking sound of a lever being worked, and the whirr of the sharp blades as they cut through thick branches of oak and pine. *A wood chipper!* He knew almost instantly. He remembered Tommy telling him about seeing one on a field at the university. *He's brought me out here to get rid of me and no one knows where I am. Jesus!*

Gary wanted to be brave. He wanted to figure a way out of this predicament. But right now he was afraid he was going to lose control of his bladder. *What a horrible way to die,* he thought, *and how pitiful to go out with wet pants.*

CHAPTER TWENTY-SEVEN

Known as "The Brute" for its capacity to process whole trees, the eighteen-inch capacity brush chipper had a powerful 180 horse-power engine. Field-tested in Australia in 2006 with whole eucalyptus trees, it passed with flying colors turning even the biggest logs into mulch in a matter of minutes. Hector Castillo's idea to use it to get rid of Gary was not a particularly novel one. Wood chippers had been suspected in the disappearance of several people over the past fifty years, including the late Teamster's Union chief, Jimmy Hoffa. A poultry plant in California recently used one to dispose of 10,000 diseased chickens, while they were still alive.

Gary was weak and nauseous from the head wound, the bruising ride, and the gas fumes that he had been breathing for the past half hour. His arms were numb and he could not even shrug his shoulders without setting off a vicious headache that left his stomach churning. He offered up a prayer for courage and gritted his teeth. He had come too far to die like this.

Up on Memorial Boulevard, Tommy had gone by the real estate office to catch up with Gary after the AA meeting. There, he learned from Victoria's personal assistant that Gary had left just minutes ago. When Tommy walked outside he saw the green pickup, which he had

161

spotted earlier at the Salve Regina soccer field. It was pulling out of the driveway with what appeared to be a bound body in the back. He rushed back inside, persuaded Oliver it was a police emergency, called 911 and asked to be connected to Lt. McGuire. The dispatcher said she couldn't do that, but she would leave a message for him. Knowing he had wasted precious minutes, he hung up, got out Officer Rego's card and called him on his cell. Rego, who'd been only three blocks away, came skidding to a stop in front of the realty office within minutes.

"What's going on?"

"I just saw the green pickup with that ugly-looking Latino guy. He had someone trussed up in the bed of the truck. Someone in clothes like Gary was wearing his morning: white shirt, green sweater and chinos. As a matter of fact, though I couldn't see his face. I'd swear it was Gary."

"Get in! Get in!" Rego shouted as he drove the car up Memorial Boulevard and hit his emergency flasher and the siren to clear traffic. He made a reckless left turn against the light onto Belleview and headed down the wide avenue as pedestrians leaped to safety and cars swerved out of the way.

Tommy suggested they head to the university, so they made a left turn on Narragansett and down to Ochre Point. They saw and heard nothing except cars pulling out of their path as the patrol's siren echoed through the quiet university.

Gary was determined not to go easily. He had been squirming in the back of the pickup as the shredder's high-powered engine revved up. He had not managed to loosen the tape binding his hands, but had been able to manipulate his feet over one of the surplus tanks in the back of the pickup. Sloshing fuel had weakened the adhesive, and he had already worked one foot partially free when Castillo lowered the back ramp of the pickup, grabbed him under his arms and dragged him over to the wood chipper. Gary thought he could hear a police siren in the distance, but it was far away--too far away, he suspected, to be of any help.

Gary pretended to still be unconscious as Castillo dragged him over the field toward the giant machine. He kept his eyes partially closed, squinting through his eyelids to take in his surroundings. The single-axle vehicle had a cavernous opening in the back, where whole trees were fed into its maw and drawn into rotating blades by a hydraulic feeder. Above it was a huge chute where the debris the monster spit out could be fed into the back of a pickup or a dumpster. Although Gary couldn't see it, it sounded like the shredder was hooked up to an older-model truck whose engine was running.

Meanwhile, Rego slowed down on Ochre Court as he and Tommy looked from side to side for any sign of the green pickup. It was nowhere in sight.

"Wait! You hear that? Turn off the siren," Tommy said.

"What? What do you hear?"

"It sounds like the motor on one of those tree chippers. You know the big ones that take whole trees and stumps. I saw one the other day. As a matter of fact, that's where I saw that Latino guy I told you about yesterday. Take a right up here on Sheppard."

Castillo was out of shape, and the effort of dragging Gary's dead weight was getting to him. His breaths were coming in sharp guttural bursts, and he was cursing.

Meanwhile Gary had heard the siren's dying drone and knew that either the cruiser had stopped somewhere too far to be of any use, or had gone off in another direction. He was on his own. No one would arrive in time to save him.

He bided his time until they were at the lip of the feeder. As Castillo bent to shove him head first into the stainless steel maw, Gary spun around, and kicked him in the chest. The blow sent Castillo careening but he didn't go down. Scrambling around him, Gary kicked again and Castillo fell backwards losing his balance. His jacket caught on the conveyor belt, and he twisted in stunned surprise, then starting screaming as the powerful hydraulic belt propelled him inexorably toward the blades. The dull metallic odor of blood filled the air, as the Bolivian's body was turned to pulp and bone meal, while his blood rose in a pink mist over the exhaust.

Rego pulled his cruiser onto the field, and sprinted from his vehicle before it stopped rolling. He hit the emergency power switch to shut down the engine on the shredder, but it was already much too late. He walked over and cut Gary's bindings.

"Jesus, what a mess!" he said. Then, while Tommy threw his arm around Gary's shoulders and helped him catch his breath, Rego radioed in for an ambulance and an investigative team. Meanwhile the air grew chilly with a taste of autumn in the air. The sky opened up, and a brief shower washed the blood off the yellow engine that was cooling down with the gentle tick-tick of a well-maintained and predictable machine.

CHAPTER TWENTY-EIGHT

Gary and Tommy were having a late breakfast at the Ocean Breeze when McGuire walked in. He threw the newspaper down on the table.

"Open it up to page three, my boys. Then read it and weep."

Gary opened the paper to the headline at the bottom of page three. He turned the paper so that Tommy could read along from the other side of the table.

MAN KILLED IN LOCAL WOOD CHIPPER ACCIDENT

Police officials, the county examiner and safety investigators are calling the death of a local landscaper—who fell into a wood chipper while feeding the machine branches on a local field yesterday—an unfortunate industrial accident.

The mutilated remains of 43 year-old Cesar Castillo of Middletown were discovered by Newport Police Officer C. Rego at the soccer field between Victoria and Shepard Avenues. The grisly scene was cordoned off by police.

Officer Rego, who was the first responder to the scene, said that he discovered the body with the engine of the full-sized commercial chipper still running. He said he immediately hit the power switch but that it was too late to save the landscape worker.

Representatives from the contracted landscape company, S & J Tree Services of Middletown, said that Castillo had been with the company only a short time, and should not have been operating the machinery without a helper.

Safety experts checked the machine, a Model 1980XP Brush Chipper which has the strength to process whole trees, and declared it to be perfectly safe when used according to the manufacturer's instructions. There were no apparent defects. The powerful chipper, which weighs about 9,000 pounds and has a 180 horsepower engine, is customarily operated by two men.

Investigators from the Rhode Island Occupational Health and Safety Administration reviewed the scene of the incident this morning and concluded that the death was accidental, ruling out criminal activity or product liability. (Story cont. on page 7).

Gary shook his head, "I can't believe this! They're passing the whole thing off as an accident?"

"Oh, it gets better, my friend," McGuire smiled grimly. "Turn to the next page where the story continues."

WOOD CHIPPER ACCIDENT Cont. from page 3

A total of 36 people have died in wood chipper accidents between 1998 and 2007 according to a 2008 Journal of the American Medical Association (JAMA) report. Mobile wood chippers are used to shred branches into mulch. Branches are fed into rotating blades which quickly crush the wood. It is an efficient way to reduce heavy branches and, in the case of larger machines such as the one in yesterday's accident, even whole trees, into tiny pieces. According to the JAMA report, the machinery can pose a danger to workers who may be pulled into the rotating blades or be struck by the machine's hood if it is being opened or closed while the blades are still moving.

The large heavy-duty brush chipper involved in this latest accident is appropriately named "The Brute" because of its additional power. A factory representative at the East Providence outlet which sells and leases the machine says that the company regrets the unfortunate accident but that the machine is perfectly safe when used in conformity with the manufacturer's instructions. (Story cont. on page 11).

Gary turned the page again, shaking his head. The newspaper was so full of advertisements that even a short news story such as this one had to be cut up into three pieces. News, it seemed, was less important than commerce. He almost failed to find the rest of the story buried beneath an ad for a new condominium complex planned in Middletown.

ACCIDENT, cont. from page 7.

This makes the third accidental death on the Island in the past year. The others were Michael Regan, a 64 year-old college professor who fell to his death off the cliffs near Rough Point, and 19 year-old Juan Miguel Andrade who died of an apparent drug overdose.

"Son-of-a-bitch!" Gary yelled, causing several of the Ocean Breeze customers to turn and frown and the manager to give him a cautioning look. Swearing and loud talk was not tolerated on Lower Thames Street. "I don't believe this! They're treating both my Dad's death and the Guatemalan kid's as accidents?"

"My guess," McGuire said, "is that we're seeing the Governor's deft hand pulling the strings once again. He doesn't want Victoria's real estate business to be hurt by FBI violent crime statistics. By passing these off as accidents, he helps maintain high property values on the Island. Crime statistics are reported on most Internet sites nowadays along with a formula which gives a crime score to every community in the U.S. The lower the score is, the more attractive the community to live in."

"Wheels within wheels. Tell me, is there anything the Governor and his gang do not have their hands in? What's next?"

"Well," McGuire announced grimly, "there is a bit more. One of the bikers we arrested, a subject by the name of James 'Fats' McIlhenny, confessed to killing the Andrade boy. He said he was paid by our deceased Bolivian. However, McIlhenny was given immunity by the DEA for providing information on his Oxycotin and cocaine connections and was removed to a federal holding facility in Providence."

"So, let me see if I can guess what comes next," Gary offered. "Officially the murder didn't take place since the killer is not formally charged with it. Thus, another violent crime statistic is unreported. Plus, I assume his assault against Tommy was also dropped as part of the plea agreement, so that will not be reported either?"

"That's almost it," McGuire nodded, "but not quite all. When Fats McIlhenny was removed to the federal holding facility, the Aryan Brotherhood killed him for being a snitch."

"Finally! We have a reportable murder," Gary grumbled. "I was beginning to think the whole State of Rhode Island would come clean."

"Well, actually the whole State *does* come clean," McGuire said ruefully. "The murder took place in a federal facility, not a state one. As such it will be included in the national statistics but not as a Rhode Island murder. It is one that took place in a U.S. detention center, and as such is treated much like one that occurs on any federal reservation."

"My God, what's next? I keep thinking that this is like one of those stories kids write in junior high that ends with the main character waking up from a dream!"

McGuire shook his head, unwilling or unable to offer Gary any condolences. Tommy sat uncomfortably sipping his coffee, wishing that the Ocean Breeze didn't have a no-smoking policy. He was just about to excuse himself and go outside for a cigarette when the elegantly-attired Jim Sloan, Attorney-at-Law, came breezing into the restaurant. He greeted the manager with a pleasant smile and a comment about the Red Sox, and then strode over to their table. He ordered a coffee from the waitress and then shook hands all around.

"No news on the wife yet, Gary, but I have assurances from the very highest authorities that everything that can be done is being done." He winked. "And every string that can be pulled is being pulled."

"Jesus. I am so sick of strings being pulled, that I could puke," Gary said. "But I suppose I should be grateful in this case. What's going on?"

Sloan turned to Tommy and McGuire and they both understood that Sloan wanted to be alone with his client.

"I need to be checking in with the station, Gary. Call me later," McGuire said. He left a ten dollar bill and headed for the door.

Tommy excused himself to go out and have a cigarette. Now it was just Gary alone with the lawyer.

"So what happens next, in this ongoing saga?" Gary asked. "I already saw the newspaper. My father's murder didn't happen. The Guatemalan kid's murder didn't happen. Now the biker's murder didn't happen. This is getting truly Orwellian. Murder is accident; falsity is truth; fiction is reality. Where do we go with this? Do you think the Civil Rights Commission or the FBI will investigate if we request it?"

"Look, Gary. It's time for you to let all this go. Justice has been served."

"What? Are you crazy, Jim? How has justice been served? Everything has been covered up, manipulated and turned on its head. The master puppeteer, the Governor, is still pulling strings. The exploitive agribusinesses rake in their profits as usual. Victoria's real estate business makes its obscene commissions as usual. Meanwhile indigenous people continue to be enslaved in Bolivia, and the dead cry out for retribution with no one to hear them."

"Do you remember the play *Romeo and Juliet*, Gary? Yes? Do you remember at the end the Prince says, *All are punishèd*? That is what has happened here. Yes, it is a tragedy. But let's look at the results. All *have* been punished. Your grandmother, who brought the young killer into the country, is now in St. Clare's Home and will be there for the rest of her life. She is an invalid as a result of her inadvertent role in all of this. That's one." He enumerated the first case on his finger and then continued counting.

"The Guatemalan boy who killed your father is himself now dead. That's two. The biker who engineered that death was killed by his own people. Three. The Bolivian capo who hired him met a horrible end in a wood chipper. That's four. All have been punished, Gary. To push any more won't bring closure or justice to anyone. It won't bring your father back. It will simply tarnish Newport's reputation, and hurt its good people, like the fellow who runs this restaurant and the waitresses who work for him, folks who work hard to maintain their homes, are proud of their community, and try to live decently."

"Fine, but what's next?" Gary asked, unwilling to accept what the persuasive lawyer told him, but not quick or articulate enough to formulate a response.

"Tonight there will be a meeting at the Hyatt Regency out on Goat Island to summarize all of these events for the press."

"A whitewashed summary, no doubt," Gary replied cynically. "And what about Victoria and her corporate client? What about the Governor? He was behind the scenes manipulating everybody with his money and his connections. Is he just going to walk away unscathed, like Doris Duke, protected by his position in society?"

"Money and connections are what the system is all about, Gary. That's how America works, and Newport is a microcosm of America at its best. If you don't like it, you're free to return to Mexico, or take up where your father left off in Bolivia. But in the meantime, be grateful to the Governor. He's working behind the scenes to get your wife back. If you want that to happen, just go to the meeting tonight and try to keep your mouth shut."

CHAPTER TWENTY-NINE

The Hyatt Regency is one of the most elegant hotels in Newport. Remote from the city and accessible only by boat or via the causeway to exclusive Goat Island, it was now in the process of a $10 million restoration. There were rolls of new carpet and sound-proofing material stacked in the lobby as they passed through on their way to the Waterfront Pavilion where the meeting was to be held.

Gary and Tommy had arrived with Jim Sloan in his town car, driven by his loyal factotum, a garrulous Irishman by the name of Sean Casey, who had kept them entertained most of the way with stories about Newport politicians from past eras.

At the front of the pavilion was a dais flanked by an American flag and the blue and white flag of Rhode Island, with its anchor and motto of "Hope" which stuck Gary as ironically appropriate. There were several dignitaries seated up there, including the chief of police, the bishop, former Governor Whitman, Newport's mayor and city manager, a naval officer in whites with gold braid, and Brigadier Hector Domínguez dressed in civilian clothes. There were several other men in Brooks Brothers and Armani suits that Gary did not recognize. He spotted Officer Rego in his dress blues, the McGuires, and some local officials seated up front. Outside the sun's last rays glinted on Narragansett Bay and a gentle light shone through the windows onto the podium.

A Hyatt employee ushered them to seats toward the front in the reserved section. There were television cameras set up, print reporters juggling notebooks and handheld recorders, and radio people with boom mikes. After making their way through the media tangle, they took their seats.

"Who are all the suits?" Gary asked Jim Sloan, nodding toward the dais.

Sloan leaned toward him and spoke *sotto voce*. "The dapper fellow in the pin-striped Armani next to the Chief is the DEA commander for this district. Seated next to the Governor is the regional director of Homeland Security. On the other side is the head of the FBI's organized crime task force. Next to him is the commandant of the State Police. The rear admiral at the end of the dais is dean of the War College."

By now there were over a hundred people in the room as the scheduled time of eight p.m. drew near. The city manager introduced the entire dais and each man stood and nodded gravely as the audience politely applauded.

"Thank you very much, ladies and gentlemen. Thank you for coming out this evening for this very important meeting. Most of you have a good idea of what this meeting is about. So, without further ado, I'm going to turn the mike over to Brad Prendergast, Special Supervisory Agent for the FBI and currently Regional Director of the Organized Crime Task Force for the Eastern Region. Brad?"

Prendergast was a serious and efficient administrator. He was dressed in a conservative navy pinstripe, black shoes and a white shirt with a burgundy tie. His hair was trimmed short in the FBI fashion and he radiated efficiency and good sense. He nodded his thanks to the city manager for the introduction, and then proceeded to outline the purpose of the meeting.

"There are a number of issues affecting this community today and because of that I've invited all interested parties as well as community leaders, the press, and local citizens to be present tonight. This is an open meeting which I hope will bring you all up-to-date and satisfy the press as well. Let me summarize what we know about several occurrences over the past two weeks. I'll begin with certain untimely deaths. First, there was the death by misadventure of Michael Regan, a visiting professor at the Pell Center. Second, we have the drug overdose of one Juan Miguel Andrade, a 19 year-old Guatemalan refugee. Third, we have the accidental death of a Bolivian landscape worker."

Gary began to raise his hand to object to the description of 'accidental' as applied to these deaths, but a hard elbow in the ribs from Jim Sloan dissuaded him.

"After a series of intensive investigations on the part of local, county and state agencies, as well as the FBI, DEA and OSHA, it has been determined that these deaths were non-criminal in origin, and thus have not been recorded on the national database. So, for civic leaders to whom such statistics are, as we all know, extremely vital for the city's economic prosperity, we are pleased to announce that for purposes of FBI national crime data, none of these deaths will be reported. Thus, the number of murders on Aquidneck Island for this year is, once again, zero. Congratulations!"

The people on the dais, none more enthusiastic than the city manager, led the audience in a round of applause.

"Next, we come to the matter of apprehending outside groups attempting to bring dangerous drugs onto the Island. I'd like to let my colleague William Stanton of the DEA address that vital issue."

Stanton, a former field agent, was beefy but stylish in a Brooks Brother blazer and tan slacks. He had risen to his position by gathering as much information as he could about every operation in the region and making friends with the federal ADA's who prosecuted his cases. Stanton exuded confidence and had an amiable air which suggested that not only was he was good at his job but that he enjoyed it. He carried a large manila folder and a small box to the podium. He took his time placing them carefully in front of him, and then he looked down at the reserved section where Tommy and Gary were seated.

"At this time," he said, "I'd like to remind you all of something that we often have a tendency to forget. We know that the war on drugs cannot be stopped by simply hiring more federal agents or by passing tougher laws and imposing longer prison sentences. It is a community problem and must be solved *in* the community, with local police and citizens working together.

"Every once in a while, we find ordinary men and women standing shoulder to shoulder with the police, risking their lives to get the poison off the streets. One such case stands out.

"On August 16th of this year, a civilian by the name of Tommy Sullivan, in concert with NPD Officer Clem Rego, was able to intercept a shipment of drugs brought onto the Island by an outlaw biker gang, appropriately named the Devil's Disciples. Officer Rego was able, after an armed struggle, to disarm these suspects and place them under arrest. The suspects subsequently led the DEA to their source which resulted in a large recovery of cocaine, OxyContin and other dangerous drugs, as well as weapons, and a significant cache of U.S. currency.

"In the course of this action, both Officer Rego and Mr. Sullivan risked their lives. Mr. Sullivan was, in fact, brutally assaulted and suffered head injuries as a result of the attack. I would like to ask Mr. Sullivan to come up to the podium at this time. Officer Rego, would you join him?"

Tommy got up from his seat a bit nonplussed by the attention and the applause which followed.

"Thomas Sullivan," Stanton intoned, opening the box he had set on the podium. "On behalf of a grateful government I would like to present you with the Meritorious Service Citation, the highest civilian award offered by this agency."

He gave Tommy the medal and shook his hand. Tommy turned to leave but Stanton touched his sleeve. He smiled when Tommy turned around. "In addition, I would also like to present you with this check for $45,000 which represents your share of the confiscation fee for cash recovered from seizures in this case. Congratulations."

When the applause died down he continued. "Officer Rego, I have asked your Chief to join us at the podium. I have a check for you as well, and the Distinguished Service Award for Law Enforcement," he said, handing Rego both the citation and the check. "But I believe you will enjoy even more what is behind curtain number two. Chief?"

The Chief came over and nodded to a Hyatt employee who pulled a cord revealing a 2006 Harley Davidson motorcycle, polished cobalt blue with shining chrome pipes. Rego recognized the bike as the 'soft-tail hog' that the Ho Chi Ming biker had been riding. It had been repainted and polished until it gleamed. It was in pristine condition and he knew that it was worth more than $30,000. *A nice present*, he thought. *Drug confiscation sure is a profitable business.*

"As part of the seizure by the government and the City of Newport, we have agreed that this confiscated Harley is an appropriate vehicle for you to have in the pursuit of your duties in and around the city. I don't think anyone will object if you cruise around on the weekends as well. You've earned it, plus it might make the next group of bikers think twice before they invade our town," he ended laughing. The crowd joined him in the laugher while giving him and Rego a round of warm applause.

"Thank you, folks. But we're not quite done yet. Clem, I have here two sets of chevrons which go along with your appointment to sergeant. Congratulations!" When the applause finally died down and Tommy and Rego returned to their seats, the Chief made his final announcement.

"I have one more promotion that I would like to announce. Pete McGuire, come on up here with your lovely wife Carolina!" He then presented McGuire with a set of captain's bars for his "diligent work in investigation above and beyond the duties of his office."

"Christ," Gary muttered to Sloan. "This is worse than the Academy Awards."

Sloan appeared composed and smiled broadly. "Ah, Gary. As they say in show business, 'you ain't seen nothing yet.'"

Stanton, meanwhile, had returned to the podium and introduced Kevin Maloney, the regional director of Homeland Security. He then announced that Brigadier General Hector Domínguez and now-Captain Pete McGuire were both on loan to Homeland Security for an indefinite period. "They will be actively engaged in investigating international corporations which have offices in the U.S. and Bolivia, whom we believe have been involved in land fraud, bribery of public officials, and collusion to effect unlawful imprisonment and slavery of Bolivian nationals."

Sloan turned to Gary. "Satisfied? Or is there possibly something more that might make the ending even more Dickensian?"

"You don't mean?"

He looked up and saw that both the FBI regional director and the Governor were smiling at him. The Director turned to the Governor. "Governor, once again, we'd like to thank you for all your help in resolving these issues. You are one of the finest examples of statesmanship and public service that Rhode Island has produced in the past four hundred years.

"Gary Regan," continued the FBI director speaking to Gary in the front row, "we gratefully acknowledge your help as well." Now he projected his voice to the rear of the audience. "Some of you may have heard that Gary has been separated from his wife during this ordeal and for the past three days, as she has been tangled up in the labyrinth of international visas and other bureaucratic complexities. Well, tonight, thanks to Governor Whitman and the staff at Homeland Security, we have a special surprise for Gary."

He nodded to the rear entrance and everyone turned in their seat as the Hyatt manager dramatically opened the wide doors. Gary's wife, Teresa, looking as if she just stepped out of a fashion magazine, entered to the applause of the crowd which rose to their feet in welcome.

CHAPTER THIRTY

Teresa and Gary spent most of the night recounting their adventures. Tommy had moved his few belongings out and had taken a room at the Hyatt for the weekend. He had made arrangements to rent a furnished apartment on Broadway with some of the reward money.

The Governor had asked them to have brunch with him in the morning but Gary was reluctant to go. Teresa insisted.

"He did manage to have my passport expedited and get me into the country," Teresa reminded him. "We owe him at least the courtesy of accepting his invitation."

"Maybe so," Gary conceded. "But most of the complications that led to my father's death, the death of the Guatemalan boy, even my grandmother's stroke, can be laid at his doorstep. It was as a result of his manipulations, his string pulling, that all these things came about."

Teresa hugged him and rested her chin on his shoulders. She loved Gary and she knew he felt strongly about being used, about being treated as a pawn by someone more powerful. Still, simple justice required that she also be honest.

"I don't know, Gary. It's kind of like saying that the gun commits the murder, or the car causes the accident. What has the

Governor really done? He only served as a means to help people secure what he thought they wanted. He helped your father get to Newport so that he could present his ideas about globalization. He helped your grandmother get amnesty for her maid's cousin. He helped your Aunt Victoria do a favor for an important client. None of these things were in themselves evil, or even wrong. He helped me get my passport so that I could get into the country and be reunited with you. It is what people have done as a result of his help that seems to be the problem. And surely, he's not responsible for that."

When the Governor's limousine arrived at 10 a.m. to take them to brunch, Teresa had almost, but not quite, persuaded Gary of the moral relativity of the Governor's acts. While he was willing to listen to any justification that the Governor might offer, it was hard for him to believe that someone could simply be a power broker, with no hidden motives.

"Governor," he asked as they were driving down Broadway. "Tell me, what gives you so much authority in so many circles? I mean, you're an ex-governor now. You have no political office. You come from old money, true. But you're no Bill Gates, you're no billionaire. There are many richer than you."

The Governor smiled. "People such as yourself, Gary, often confuse authority with power, or money with power. Presidents, senators, all have *authority*. The prestige of their office, the title that goes with it, both carry authority. But as most first-term senators learn, authority is nothing without the *power* to exercise it. If you can't get the votes to have your bill passed, if you can't influence others to follow your lead, then the authority you have is papier-mâché. What I have is something different. What I have is the power that comes from connections, from favors done, from obligations incurred by anyone who received those favors.

"Another mistake is thinking that money gives you power. Hell, there are many millionaires, even billionaires, who have less than a tenth of the power I have. Their money is new, their connections are weak; they've spent money solely on themselves and their own businesses and concerns. Society owes them nothing. They can only buy what their money allows them to buy. No more. On the other hand, my money and my influence are part of every construction project, every zoning waiver, and every restoration effort in this city. My family's money has provided jobs and income and even housing to ten generations of residents on this island. And it continues to do so."

The chauffeur took a left off Broadway onto Admiral Kalbfus Road, crossed Malbone, and pulled up to the Newport Grand, the monumental casino complex close to the city limits. Gary was surprised. He thought that they would be going to some place more secluded and elegant. The Grand, despite its name, smacked of quick money, hustle, and get-rich-quick dreams of tourists.

When they entered the casino, Gary was overwhelmed by the hundreds of slot machines, the roulette tables, and the poker and dice games. He saw the haze of smoke rising from the dozens of ashtrays next to the active slot machines. He looked over at Teresa.

Teresa shook her head. "I thought that smoking was forbidden by ordinance anywhere in the city," she said. "How can they get away with this here?"

"Ironic, isn't it?" the Governor remarked. "You see how laws can be bent or even circumvented? You can't smoke in any restaurant or bar in Newport, but you can smoke in the casino. Why, you wonder? It's because the income generated by this place, which supplements the education budget and improves infrastructure, far outweighs the so-called health issues of second-hand smoke. The same is true of Las Vegas, by the way. A glassed-in non-smoking section with purified air is provided for non-smokers, but the die-hard smokers are encouraged to come here and spend their money. In fact, smokers are more welcome than others because their sort of risk-taking behavior often causes them to bet their entire paychecks with an eye on the jackpot."

"Speaking of jackpots," Teresa, said, "this is a pretty good one."

Gary looked over at the traditional slot machines and the more elaborate video slots. There were patrons of all ages and descriptions busy playing Wheel of Fortune, Cash Fever and Cleopatra, betting with both tokens and card credits. Above one row of games which included Treasure of Avalon, Presto and Chambers of Gold were the flashing lights of the CA$HOLA jackpot now recording a total payout of $360,000 and rising.

"Enough money to buy a simple Cape Cod cottage on one of the back streets of Newport," the Governor noted casually. "The same kind of house a working class family might have bought in the Fifties for $20,000. So much for modern jackpots and fortunes. And the Grand will extract a couple of million in workers' paychecks and old folks' retirement benefits before anyone collects the big payout."

In the casino restaurant Gary and the Governor both had omelets while Teresa had the stuffed quahogs and fries. The food at the restaurant was surprisingly good, and Gary commented on the fact.

"It is also plentiful and inexpensive," the Governor added. "The management wants customers to feel like they are being treated well, catered to, taken care of, and not being ripped off. No petty charges, no hustling you for tips. There are also free soft drinks and coffee, and inexpensive rooms in the motel across the street if you want to stay over to get an early start on gambling the next day.

"It's part of the Great American Illusion. None of the people here consider themselves to be poor, despite the fact that many are on fixed income, or living from paycheck to paycheck. They all believe that they are potentially rich. If you're *really* rich, you know it. If you're *potentially* rich, they'll treat you like you're rich even after you lose all your money, so you'll keep coming back to lose more.

"When I was a kid," the Governor continued, "there were the upper classes, old money people, and the middle classes which included merchants, doctors and lawyers. All the rest were working class from policemen to teachers, stone masons to plumbers. Now everyone is middle class with dreams of becoming upper class. With no solid working class base, the Democratic Party has effectively disappeared. Everyone is some kind of Libertarian which is just what the corporations want. Individual consumers with no sense of social solidarity, isolated and greedy, with their votes for sale to whoever promises to keep them safe. They think that government is something like hotel management. If taxes are low, inflation is controlled, immigrants and minorities are locked up, then everything is fine. No one cares about freedom, about democracy, or about leaving their homes, getting away from the iPods, cell phones and laptops, to serve the community and build human solidarity."

Teresa objected. "I think people can make a difference. We can still vote; we can change a government that does not serve our interests."

"You think so, Teresa? You think it makes any difference whom you elect when the winner will always be someone who has raised the $400 million in cash to run the campaign, and made another $20 billion in promises to get corporate backing? There's a new world government and it's not composed of Bush, or Clinton, Obama or Chávez or any government. It's made up of international corporations like British Petroleum, Time-Warner, Raytheon, General Electric, Mitsubishi, and Dow Chemical. They tell governments what to do, where to invest, who to run for office. They have their own security which they lease out to governments when a country's army is too weak or overextended to do the job, as we have seen with Blackwater, the security provider in Iraq. They control the airports, marine transport, communication, satellites and surveillance. They also tell us which countries to invest in and which countries are too risky. They even determine which governments will last and which ones will fail. The top twenty corporations have more resources and power than the U.S., Russia, Germany and Japan put together. Don't fool yourself that you're living in a democracy. The only consolation is—nobody else in the world is living in one either."

The Governor paid the bill and they followed him to the front door where the chauffeur waited with the limousine. They got themselves seated as he gave the driver instructions.

"One more side trip before I take you home. This one will illustrate an important aspect of Newport. But not just Newport, of American society as a whole."

As they turned off Van Zandt Avenue onto Broadway headed back to downtown, Gary looked out the window at the traffic and was suddenly at a loss for words. Teresa was silent as well. Neither one of them had offered a rebuttal to the Governor's remarks. Gary couldn't even clearly articulate what he was feeling. Confusion? Frustration? What the Governor said went against most of Gary's most cherished instincts and beliefs, yet he felt that the Governor was right. He suspected, by Teresa's silence, that she felt the same. He reached over and clasped her hand.

The chauffeur tuned off Broadway, down Warner to Farewell Street. The latter was appropriately named since it was the site of the city's oldest and most populous graveyard. The driver parked on the grass lip bordering the street and then came around the car. He let the Governor out first, and then opened the rear door for Teresa and Gary.

They hiked up to the entrance of the Common Burial Ground while the Governor began some pleasant tourist-guide chatter. "This is an important landmark," he said. "A colonial governor is buried here, also a signer of the Declaration of Independence." He pointed out some of the elaborate gravestones and monuments to early merchants and sea captains. "And over in this section," he said, pointing to broken slate of several old tombs, "is what we call 'God's Little Acre.' Here are buried former slaves and African freemen who lived and worked and died in the early colony. They are commemorated along with the rich and powerful, although with less pomp or ceremony."

"Very interesting, Governor," Gary snapped. "But what's the point? Teresa and I both have things to do." By now the wind had picked up and Gary felt a chill in the air as he put his arm around his wife.

"The point is that when we look at the history of who we were as a people, what stands out is that we honored the *individual*. In life, in death, well *after* death, even the most humble found their place in American society. That's who we *were*. Now, we cremate the bodies and their children toss their ashes into the sea, or the widow scatters them on her flower beds. This generation cares nothing for history, and nothing for the people who made this city. It is a generation without honor, without values. They did away with form, believing that substance was more important. But without form, you have no substance. They did away with courtesy and put political correctness in its place, without realizing that courtesy is the glue that holds a society together. It is a generation of people who care only for themselves. They've replaced intimacy and caring with Internet video games and pornography."

"What the hell do video games and pornography have to do with anything?" Gary asked, becoming impatient now and thinking: *Finally the old man is going senile.* "Plus, I don't think you're the person to lecture us on intimacy and caring."

"Perhaps not. But when the Nazis decided to take over Poland, the first thing they did was to saturate the country with pornography and to make it legal. They knew that once men could visualize women or boys as objects to be manipulated, they could see Jews as objects as well. It is no small leap. You think that you're morally superior to the Nazis but in fact this generation has replicated exactly what occurred in Poland only on a much larger scale. People in this new generation see everyone else as objects which exist simply as means to their personal ends. That's why there is no more democracy in America. Democracy means working with others to accomplish an end that is larger than yourself. It means working side by side to establish a just and caring society."

"And did you try to do that? Did these merchants and sea captains who had slaves try to do that?"

"Well Gary, most of us, including my ancestors who are buried here, would say that indeed we did. A fair reading of history would suggest that we created a more just society than existed before we came to this country. But this generation's lack of respect for that effort, or lack of honor for what was created, has turned the whole country into a marketplace where goods and services and people are sold for a price, used up, and then tossed on the garbage heap to be disposed of."

"So what is your point, exactly?" Teresa asked. She was chilled now and anxious to get back to the warmth of the car.

"Well, my dear, I brought you here so that you and Gary could see how much history this island has. How this old island will outlive us all. And how history is defined not by what happened, but by how we choose to regard what happened. I am aware that Gary inherited money from his father. I know it will give you both time to sort things out, time for Gary to finish his father's manuscript. Time even for Gary to write a book of his own."

"Oh, I intend to, Governor. I intend to write a book about all of this; you can be sure of that."

"Well, if you do, Gary, I suggest that you make it a novel. The facts are so tangled that you'll never unravel them enough to make a believable history. As a novel, it could be interesting. But whether it is interesting like *Payton Place*, or interesting like *Crime and Punishment* depends to a great extent on whether you're real, or whether you're like the disposable people who end up with their ashes scattered in their widows' rhododendrons and nothing to show for their brief sojourn on earth.

Gary took Teresa's hand and walked toward the opening in the ancient stone walls. He turned to see the Governor staring distractedly at a chipped monument of a colonial governor. He called to him. "Tell your driver to go ahead without us, Governor. Teresa and I will walk home. And by the way, Governor, when I do write my novel, you can be sure of a featured role."

The Governor looked up, his thinning gray hair tossed by the wind, his faded blue eyes still fierce and clear. "I wouldn't have it any other way, Gary. Just make sure you capture my charm."

ENVOI

When they returned to the apartment, Gary found a note from Tommy on the kitchen counter thanking Gary for putting him up for the past week and for his help in keeping him sober. He wrote that he had found a comfortable one-bedroom apartment on Broadway, provided the address and phone number, and said that the phone would be connected by tomorrow. He ended his note with a request. "If I don't see you tonight at the meeting, call me tomorrow so I can tell you about my new job!"

"Tommy's got a new job," Gary told Teresa.

"What kind of job, I wonder?"

"No idea. But he left his phone number and said it should be in service tomorrow. We'll give him a call in the morning."

Teresa made a simple lunch of tuna salad sandwiches, tortilla chips and iced tea. When they finished, Gary headed to the fire escape to enjoy a postprandial cigarette. Teresa followed him out.

"Gary, instead of lighting that, how about we go for a tranquil walk by the cliffs? That way you'll put some healthy sea air in your lungs, and we can both let the ocean breezes blow some of the stress away."

Gary took the cigarette from between his lips and put it back into the pack. He went inside, crumpled the half-empty pack and threw it into the trash. "You're right," he said in response to her gentle hint. "It's time to put these things away for good. Let's go."

They walked together down Ruggles Avenue, past the tennis courts, the music school and the Wetmore estate. When they reached the Cliff Walk they could hear the ping of a halyard against the aluminum flagpole on the lawn of an estate to the south. The wind was picking up; fall was in the air. On their way down they had passed coeds headed for orientation at the university. It reminded Gary that classes would be starting soon and that he and Teresa would need to move out by the end of the week.

Gary felt sad to be leaving. It seemed like months had passed since he first heard of his father's untimely death and had come north in search of his killer. He reflected on his friendship with Tommy, his new insights into the convoluted history of his family, and his realization of the importance of his father's work. Then there was the funeral, the two attempts on his life, and the charade at the Hyatt.

"It's hard to believe that so much has happened in the space of only two weeks."

"I know, Teresa replied. It seem like we've been apart for months."

He gave her a hug and then clasped her hand as they continued onto the dirt path that skirted the Breakers. She looked up at him and searched his eyes.

"And what do you think all of this means for us, Gary? Where do you see us going from here? Do you really want to stay and finish your father's book? Maybe start one of your own?"

"Yes, I do," Gary said. But knowing that Teresa had her own work in Mexico, he compromised. "We don't need to be in the

States, though, for me to do that. I can write anywhere. And with computers, the Internet, I can do my research in Mexico just as easily as here."

Teresa squeezed his hand reassuringly. "But I like it here, Gary. I like the way history is still honored in this city. I like the ocean, the ease of walking or riding a bike almost anywhere, the absence of traffic jams and pollution. I even like the old Governor; he's more of a frustrated idealist than the callous cynic you make him out to be, someone who's tried to help people and make things better. Sure, he's made mistakes, but at least he hasn't spent his *whole* life just looking out for number one. He really does care for this city, for its people."

Gary checked his tongue. He didn't agree with Teresa and probably never would, but this did not seem to be an appropriate time to start an argument.

They headed down the path that would lead them past Salve Regina and take them eventually to Memorial Boulevard. They had just passed the Forty Steps when they heard a familiar voice up around the bend.

"Be careful here, ladies. This is poison ivy and as you can see it is quite a bit taller than you probably remember from your childhood. Part of the reason is global warming and the rise of CO_2. Poison ivy thrives on carbon dioxide."

They came around the corner and discovered Tommy in pressed khaki shorts and a green polo shirt lecturing a group of elderly tourists. They waited until he had finished speaking and the group began moving down the path before they approached.

Tommy greeted them enthusiastically. He pointed proudly to the City Parks and Recreation logo on his shirt. "City naturalist!" he announced. "Can you believe it?"

"So that's the new job!" Teresa grinned. "From what Gary told me about your love for plants and nature, it seems ideal."

"Congratulations, Tommy," Gary said offering his hand.

Tommy brushed the hand away and put his arms around Gary in a warm hug. "I probably wouldn't be here today, Gary, if it wasn't for you. But listen, I've got to get back to the group. See you tonight at the meeting, okay?" He hugged him a final time and then jogged ahead to catch up with the group of seniors.

"Well, Teresa smiled after Tommy left. "At least something good came out of all this. It seems that you and the Governor have something in common."

"What do you mean?" Gary said, taken aback. "What could I possibly have in common with that old man?"

"Well," Teresa persisted. "Remember that he talked about real people as opposed to disposable people. 'Real people,' he said, 'find way to help others, and are active citizens in the community.' And I think you and the Governor have both seen in the past two weeks that the real people in a society are not always who you think they are. Sometimes they seem like disposable people—like Tommy with his shopping cart and his rummaging through garbage—must have seemed. But now, because of you and Officer Rego and the head of Parks and Recreation, giving him a second chance, he's a respected guide and someone who adds to the community."

"And how about us" Gary asked.

"Oh, we're just ordinary people, like those commemorated in 'God's Little Acre.' No more, but also no less. We fill our niche and we do what we can. We could even be part of what holds it all together right here in Newport."

"And how might we do that?"

"Well, when I saw those elderly people with Tommy, I thought of a way we could make a difference. We have 1.6 million dollars in voting shares at CITCO and winter is coming soon. The least we can do is see that people on fixed incomes get cheap heating fuel. I mean if we really want to make a difference, we need to put our money where our mouth is."

"*Our* money, hey?" Gary asked. "You certainly were indoctrinated down there in Bolivia, *mi amor.*

Teresa smiled, raising her fist in the power salute, remembering Che and the dusty village south of Santa Cruz. *Viva la revolución,* she thought, then she lowered her arm and gave Gary a hug. Gary wrapped his arms around her and held her tight. A chill wind was coming in with the shuddering crash of the breakers, winter was drawing closer, but he felt only her warmth and the steady beating of her heart.

ABOUT THE AUTHOR

Michael Hogan was born in Newport, Rhode Island. His poetry has appeared in numerous periodicals including *The Paris Review*, *The Iowa Review*, *The Harvard Review*, and the *American Poetry Review*, as well as in many anthologies such as *The Pushcart Book of Poetry: The Best Poems of Thirty Years of the Pushcart Prize, ed. by Joan Murray. Pushcart Press (New York, 2006); Literature*, ed. by Robert Diyanni, Random House (New York, 2001); *Sound and Sense*, ed. by Laurence Perrine and Thomas Arp. Harcourt, Brace College Publishing (New York, 1996), and *An Introduction to Poetry*, ed. by X.J. Kennedy, Little, Brown & Co. (Boston, 1987).

His many awards include fellowships from the Alden Dow Creativity Center, the Colorado Humanities Program, and the

National Endowment for the Arts, two Pushcart Prizes, as well as the Grace Stoddard Literary Fellowship from the University of Arizona, and a career commendation for outstanding service by the Office of Overseas Schools, U.S. Department of State.

From 1990 to 2004 Hogan headed the English Department at the American School Foundation of Guadalajara, A.C., served as faculty advisor to the school's internationally recognized literary magazine, *Sin Fronteras*, and as a professor of International Relations (1996-2000) at the Autonomous University of Guadalajara. Since 2004 he has been a consultant to the College Board in Latin America, and to the U.S. Department of State's Office of Overseas Schools.

Hogan lives in Colonia Providencia, Guadalajara, with the textile artist Lucinda Mayo and their dog, Molly Malone.

OTHER WORKS BY MICHAEL HOGAN

POETRY

Letters for My Son (1975)
If You Ever Get There, Think of Me (1976)
Soon It Will Be Morning (1976)
April, 1976 (1977)
Rust (1977)
Risky Business (1978)
The Broken Face of Summer (1981)
Making Our Own Rules: Selected Poems (1978)

FICTION

A Lion At A Cocktail Party (1978)
Molly Malone and the San Patricios (1998)

NON-FICTION

Intelligent Mistakes: Grammar Supplement for Latin Americans Writing in English (1991)
The Irish Soldiers of Mexico: A History of the San Patricio Battalion (1997)
Los Soldados Irlandeses de México. Trans. by Clever Chávez Marín. (1998)
A Writers Manual for Inmates in Correctional Institutions (2001)
Teaching from the Heart: Working At International Schools in Latin America (2003)
Savage Capitalism: Latin America in the Third Millennium (2010)